The Death (and Further Adventures) of Silas Winterbottom

THE BODY THIEF

The Death (and Further Adventures) of Silas Winterbottom

The Body Thief

Stephen M. Giles

Cover design by Liz Demeter/Demeter Design

Published by Sourcebooks Jabberwocky, an imprint of Sourcebooks, Inc.
P.O. Box 4410, Naperville, Illinois 60567-4410
(630) 961-3900
Fax: (630) 961-2168
www.jabberwockykids.com

First published in Australia in 2009 by Pan Macmillan Australia.

Library of Congress Cataloging-in-Publication data is on file with the publisher.

Source of Production: Sheridan Books, Chelsea, Michigan, USA
Date of Production: August 2010
Run Number: 12849

Printed and bound in the United States of America.
SB 10 9 8 7 6 5 4 3 2 1

To my parents,
Mary & Brian,
for everything

CONTENTS

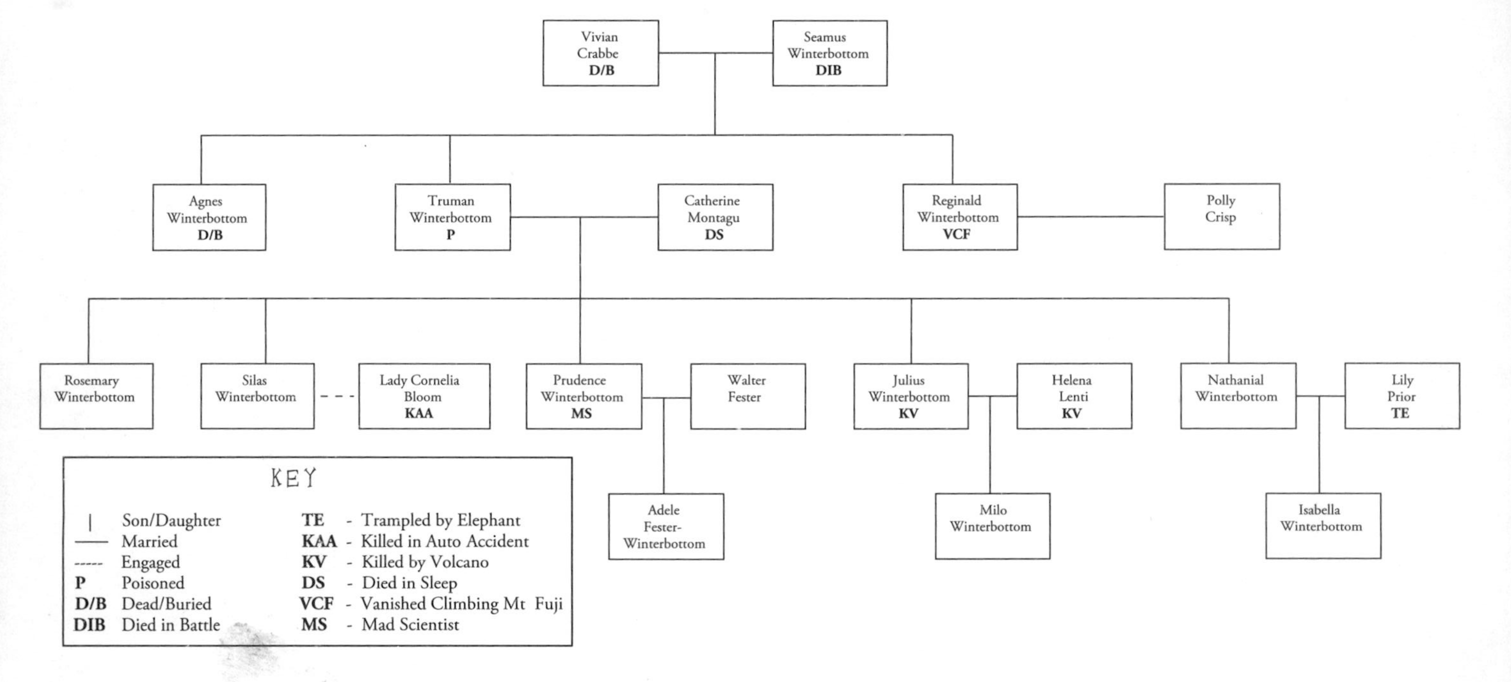
THE WINTERBOTTOM FAMILY TREE
Vivian Crabbe D/B
Seamus Winterbottom DIB
Agnes Winterbottom D/B
Truman Winterbottom P
Catherine Montagu DS
Reginald Winterbottom VCF
Polly Crisp
Rosemary Winterbottom
Silas Winterbottom
Lady Cornelia Bloom KAA
Prudence Winterbottom MS
Walter Fester
Julius Winterbottom KV
Helena Lenti KV
Nathanial Winterbottom
Lily Prior TE
Adele Fester-Winterbottom
Milo Winterbottom
Isabella Winterbottom
KEY
| Son/Daughter
—— Married
----- Engaged
P Poisoned
D/B Dead/Buried
DIB Died in Battle
TE - Trampled by Elephant
KAA - Killed in Auto Accident
KV - Killed by Volcano
DS - Died in Sleep
VCF - Vanished Climbing Mt Fuji
MS - Mad Scientist

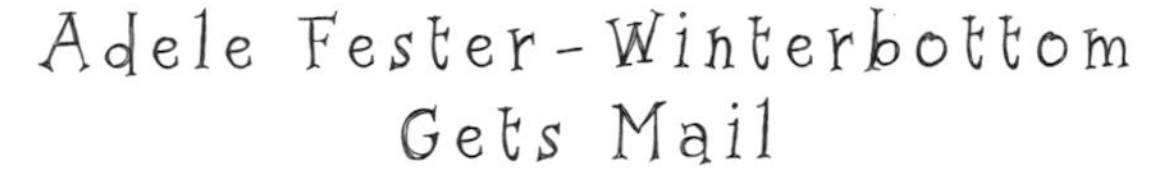

Adele Fester-Winterbottom Gets Mail

Washington, a stocky black bulldog, was licking at the saucer of milk and purring softly when Mr. Walter Fester entered the kitchen muttering to himself about the outrageous price of eggs. Washington, through no fault of his own, was a dog who firmly believed that he was a cat.

"How's a person meant to enjoy his morning eggs when they've cost him an extra fifteen cents on the dozen," said Mr. Walter Fester irritably. "You'd think we were *made* of money. I shall write to the newspaper about this. Oh, before I forget," said Mr. Fester, putting on a bright yellow apron, "this came for you."

He handed his daughter an envelope. It was royal blue with a thin silver band along the border. As letters went, it looked rather important.

"For me?" said Adele curiously.

Her mother looked up from the pages of her scientific journal. "For *her?*" She narrowed her unnaturally large eyes. "Who on earth would send Adele a letter?"

Who indeed? Adele examined the envelope in her hands. It was addressed as follows:

Miss Adele Fester-Winterbottom

399 Possum Avenue,

Tipping Point

Tasmania, Australia

On the other side, pressed into the seal of the envelope, was an engraved crest—it featured a set of ornate gates entwined with the vines of a rosebush. Etched across the crest was the word *Sommerset.*

Something about the letter made her feel nervous and excited all at once. She thought about letting her father read it for her, but Mr. Fester was busy enough scrambling eggs *and* shuffling through the sizable mountain of unpaid bills and final notices on the kitchen counter.

Back in Scotland, before everything had gone so horribly wrong, Mr. Fester had been a respected book restorer with an international reputation. It was a passion Adele had shared with her father, but now the business was long gone and there were very few books sent his way anymore.

You are probably wondering exactly what disaster befell the family to cause their complete financial ruin.

For the answer, look no further than the scrawny woman with the irritable expression and the wild mop of charcoal-colored hair sitting at the far end of the table. Adele's mother, Professor Prudence Fester-Winterbottom, was a deeply unpleasant woman with sour breath. She was also something of a genius and her specialty was animal behavior. Her groundbreaking research at MacDougall University in Edinburgh was acclaimed worldwide and over the years her reputation and public standing flourished, much to her delight.

Unfortunately, the only thing the professor craved more than glory was money. Prudence had spent a lifetime envying her older brother Silas Winterbottom and his massive fortune. So when, during an experiment into the physiology of birds, she discovered a way to dramatically alter the physical appearance of a common tree sparrow, a rather diabolical idea began to form in her mind.

The professor realized that by putting the tree sparrow through a series of rather painful and highly unethical operations she could give it the appearance of a wallop lark—the rarest bird on the face of the earth *and* the most valuable. Each feathered impostor could be sold for a small fortune.

She would be rich!

In a remote basement laboratory in the bowels of the university, the professor and her assistant Paul gathered a test group of twelve tree sparrows and began their highly unethical operation in earnest. They worked late at night to avoid detection and in no time at all had successfully created the first batch of mutant wallop larks. The professor arranged for a rather lucrative sale through a friend of Paul's who knew several notorious bird smugglers. The profit on the first dozen alone would be in excess of one hundred thousand dollars!

However, as the days passed, the birds began to exhibit rather violent tendencies not typically associated with the peaceful wallop lark. Their beaks and claws grew rapidly, sharp as razor blades, and soon all twelve birds had to be separated for fear that they would devour one another, so insatiable were their appetites.

Fearing that worst, Paul begged the professor to abandon the project and destroy the birds, but she refused, unwilling to turn her back on all of that beautiful money.

On the day of the sale, Professor Fester-Winterbottom arrived early at the university to check up on Paul, who had been working throughout the night to prepare the birds for transportation. When the professor entered the basement laboratory she made a discovery so horrific, it snatched all the strength from her legs, sending her plummeting to the ground. Paul's body lay sprawled on the floor, largely hidden beneath the swarm of rabid wallop larks devouring his flesh. With ruthless efficiency they were eating him piece by piece, stripping the bones clean.

The birds had used their powerful beaks to chew through the locks on the cages. They had waited patiently until Paul's back was turned before striking. He did not stand a chance against their savage hunger.

Unable to conceal the horror of what she had done, the professor was forced to confess everything to the university. The press jumped on the sensational story. Headlines screamed, BIRDBRAINED PROFESSOR CREATES KILLER SPARROWS!

Not surprisingly, the university was sued by Paul's grief-stricken family. In turn the university sued the professor for every penny she was worth and then some. Desperate to bury the scandal, the university convinced Scotland Yard not to pursue the case, and the investigation was quietly closed.

Not that it mattered. The professor's reputation was utterly destroyed.

Broke and desperate, Adele and her parents fled Scotland and sought refuge in the only place that would have them—Tipping Point, Tasmania.

Pushing those dark memories from her mind, Adele reached down and patted Washington on the head; the bulldog purred gratefully. Washington was an unfortunate victim of an early experiment carried out by the professor. She was convinced that she could reprogram a domesticated dog, replacing its canine instincts with those of a cat. While the experiment had been a triumph (Washington was completely transformed, purring and meowing like a lifelong fluff-ball) it quickly became apparent that the professor was unable to reverse the effects, thus condemning the stocky bulldog to life as a cat.

Adele looked again at the envelope in her hand. She felt a ripple of excitement. Who *had* written to her? With some care, she broke the seal and read the letter.

Dear Adele,

This letter may come as something of a surprise as we have never met. Time, however, is not on my side, so allow me to get straight to the point. I am dying and it is my wish that

I might get the chance to know you, at least a little, before death takes me. I would like you to be my guest at Sommerset for two months beginning in June. I have enclosed a check for $10,000 to cover the necessary travel arrangements and additional expenses. Should you accept my offer, I will expect you no later than June 1.

If the answer is no, I shall not trouble you again. The money is yours to spend in any way you wish.

Regards,
Your Uncle,
Silas Winterbottom

Adele could scarcely believe what she had just read. After some hesitation she reached into the envelope and pulled out a small rectangular piece of paper. It was a check! A check for ten thousand dollars!

Adele did not realize that she had just let out a fantastic scream, but evidently she had, for both of her parents were staring at her queerly. The professor looked irritated at the sudden outburst.

"What on earth are you shrieking about, girl?"

"Uncle Silas," said Adele, trying to suppress her mounting excitement. "It's a check from Uncle Silas!"

"Silas!" shouted the professor, her eyes bulging madly. "Did you say *Silas?* Silas Winterbottom?"

Adele nodded nervously. "That's what it says." She folded the check and quickly slid it back inside the encrusted envelope. "He is dying," she said quietly, "and he wants me to visit with him at Sommerset."

"Visit him?" said Mr. Fester anxiously.

Adele nodded. "I feel very sorry for Uncle Silas," she said, "but don't you think it is a very odd invitation considering I've never even met him before?"

The professor jumped up and slid halfway across the table, lunging for the letter.

"Of course it's not *odd!*" she said breathlessly. "It's thoughtful, that's what it is. You said something about a check—how much is it for, my dear?"

"Ten thousand dollars," Adele told her. "Silas says that if I don't wish to visit him at Sommerset, then the money is mine to keep."

Mr. Fester grinned widely. "Oh, my girl, this is great news!" he declared. "Naturally, I'd never let you go and stay with that tyrant, but just *think* of the money. Why, we could clear a few bills with ten thousand dollars."

"What?" the professor hollered. "Not let her go? Are you a complete maniac?"

"Now, Prudence, I don't like to speak badly of a sick man," said Mr. Fester carefully, "but Silas Winterbottom is the most tight-fisted, blackhearted, evil-minded scoundrel who ever lived."

The professor gasped. "Walter Fester, take that back!"

"I will not," her husband told her plainly. "Silas has never shown this family an ounce of kindness—last year when we had our *trouble*

I begged him to lend us enough money to save the house, and what did he do? He called us fools and laughed in our faces."

"Walter, try not to be such a nincompoop," suggested his wife. "Silas is dying. It stands to reason that he has invited Adele to Sommerset because he wishes to leave his fortune to her. Would you seek to deny your own daughter such an opportunity? Horrible man!"

Mr. Fester smoothed down his mustache, which he did whenever he was thinking a problem over. "Silas...he must be sitting on a tidy sum by now," he said gingerly.

"A fortune," said the professor with certainty. "A very *large* fortune."

"How did he become so rich?" said Adele, desperately hoping to discover that there was a great adventurer who struck gold or a brilliant inventor in the Winterbottom family tree.

"He married it," said the professor harshly. "Well, he was *going* to marry it. His fiancée, Lady Cornelia Bloom, died the day before they were to wed. She left the entire Sommerset estate to Silas. Foolish girl!"

"She died?" said Adele, her dark eyes wide open. "What happened to her?"

The professor shrugged. "Killed in a car accident. Silas got *everything*, including Sommerset, a magnificent estate on its very own island. Not to mention several million dollars from Lady Bloom's trust fund. Since that time, the fortune has only grown." The professor pointed triumphantly at her daughter. "And it could be all yours!"

"You're forgetting the others, Prudence," said her husband cautiously. "To begin with, there's your older brother Nathanial;

he's got a daughter around Adele's age, doesn't he? Not to mention your sister Rosemary and your brother Julius—as I recall he had a son. Gave the boy a most peculiar name."

"Rosemary hasn't been heard of in nearly twenty years," said the professor dismissively. "As for my brothers, well, yes, they each have a child. But Julius is dead, God rest his soul, and Silas has even *less* affection for Nathanial than he does for us."

As her parents discussed the likelihood of Adele inheriting a colossal fortune from an uncle she had never met, the young girl quietly packed her schoolbag, tucked her remarkably frizzy red hair firmly under her school hat, and headed for the front door.

"Wait, my dear," called her mother, following Adele into the hallway.

"You'll go, won't you?" the professor asked hopefully. "To Sommerset, I mean."

"If it's all the same to you, Mother, I'd rather not," said Adele. "I don't think I would like to go so far away all on my own."

"Well, you wouldn't be on your *own*, my dear," said the professor calmly. "Silas is family, after all."

"But he is a stranger to me," said Adele faintly. "I would much rather stay here if you don't mind."

"Of course, dear."

"Well, I better go, or I'll be late for school."

Adele had just opened the front door when she felt her mother's long spindly fingers grip her wrist, pulling her back.

"Listen to me," she hissed, her eyes glowing with fury. "You *are* going to Sommerset, and you *are* going to be the most delightful niece that any uncle could hope for. Do you understand?"

"Let me go!" said Adele, but her mother's grip only tightened, coiling around her wrist like a python choking its prey.

"There is something you should know, my dear," the professor whispered in her ear. "There is a place not a hundred miles from here called Ratchet's House. It's a *special* place for revolting little brats that nobody wants. Should you decide *not* to go to Sommerset, then I'm afraid your father and I will be forced to send you there for the foreseeable future. You see, we have so little money left and the cost of raising a twelve-year-old girl is ridiculously expensive."

Adele felt a rush of cold fear swell up in her chest. She knew of Ratchet's House from the children at school. It was a dreadful, horrid place, no better than a prison! All the windows were barred; a guard kept watch at the front gate and the whole compound was surrounded by an enormous concrete wall topped with barbed wire to prevent escape. Inmates were given only soup, bread, and apples to eat, visitors were strictly forbidden, and even the youngest of them was forced to work in the shoe factory beneath the schoolhouse every day after classes.

"You can't," Adele managed to say. "Dad would never let you send me to a place like Ratchet's House."

"Your father will do as he is told," said the professor calmly. "Oh, I am sure he will come to your defense at first and kick up a great fuss, but eventually he will accept that I know best. He always does."

The professor released her grip, leaving behind a deep red stain curling around Adele's wrist.

"The choice is yours, my dear," said the professor lightly. "If you wish to avoid Ratchet's House, then you will accept your Uncle Silas's kind offer. You are not a pretty girl, but you are clever—I am sure you will make the right choice."

Pushing past her mother, Adele stepped outside and felt the cool wind against her face. She stopped but did not turn back to look at the professor.

"All right," she said, her voice barely a whisper, "I'll go to Sommerset."

Opportunity Knocks

Dressed immaculately in a pale brown riding outfit, her hair pulled tightly back in a neat bun, Isabella Winterbottom entered the elegant cream and yellow living room of the fifth-floor apartment she shared with her father and flopped down on the plump sofa, surrounded by a dozen velvet and silk cushions.

"Horse riding is boring," she declared loudly. "Horses are boring and they poop at the most *embarrassing* moments. They're revolting!"

Isabella was a pretty girl and she knew it, with dazzling blue eyes (which she inherited from her mother, who had died tragically when Isabella was barely six months old, trampled to death by a rogue elephant while attending a disreputable traveling circus in Blackpool), creamy skin, and silky black hair (which she inherited from her father, who was very much alive).

"Would you like a glass of water, Miss Winterbottom?" called Svanhildur from the kitchen.

Svanhildur was the Winterbottom's Icelandic housekeeper—an astonishingly short woman with a sweet smile and a disturbing enthusiasm for waxing the floor.

"I'm not thirsty," replied Isabella sluggishly, stretching her legs out in front of her. She glanced around at the living room and her mood began to brighten; how different it was to the old house in Grimethorpe, which was a bleak thatched cottage sitting in an overgrown garden of weeds and rotting sunflowers. She did not like to think of how life had been back then, with no money, no joy, and most punishing of all, no beauty.

Isabella heard the front door closing and the familiar steps of her father coming down the hallway.

"Hello, princess," Mr. Winterbottom said with forced good cheer as he bent down and kissed his daughter's forehead. "What a day! I had a two-hour training session with Ralph in Hyde Park—he says I have the natural athleticism of a twenty-year-old, by the way. Then I met with Mr. Faulkner from the bank. Didn't go too well, not that I expected it would. Still, it's only money—you went riding, I see."

Isabella nodded.

"And then to lunch at your friend Amelia Vanderbolt's house?" he asked, settling into his favorite red leather armchair by the fireplace.

"That's right," said Isabella casually.

Though he was naturally quite pale, Nathanial Winterbottom was a vain man who spent many dedicated hours browning himself under the hot sun (and in winter, under the tanning bed at the Grosvenor Square Beauty Spa and Rejuvenation Clinic). As a consequence, his skin was a permanent shade of coffee brown and had the texture of a weathered coconut.

"Was your visit to the Vanderbolts' *fruitful?*"

"Of course," Isabella replied sweetly. "Amelia is so kind and the Vanderbolts always make me feel right at home." She leaned forward and retrieved a small object from inside her left riding boot, placing it on the bureau next to her father. "This must have slipped into my boot while I was admiring Mrs. Vanderbolt's jewelry box," she said. "How careless of me."

Switching on the table lamp, Nathanial picked up the delicately crafted silver watch and examined it under the light with all the skill of an experienced jeweler. It appeared to be silver. Perhaps a century old. While not a rare piece, it was sure to have some value.

"Well done, princess! I trust you were careful."

"Aren't I always?"

Her father nodded approvingly. "Did you plant a decoy?"

"Of course I did," snapped Isabella, rather offended that he even had to ask. "The Vanderbolts have a serving maid who looks completely guilty without even trying. I casually mentioned to Amelia that I spotted this particular maid coming out of Mrs. Vanderbolt's bedroom shortly after lunch. Naturally suspicion will fall to her when Mrs. Vanderbolt realizes her watch is missing."

"Good work," said Mr. Winterbottom, wrapping the watch carefully in a silk handkerchief and locking it inside the hidden compartment of the antique bureau drawer.

"How much do you think you can get for it?" Isabella asked her father.

"Hard to say," said Nathanial. He sighed. "But I doubt it will be enough to satisfy Mr. Faulkner at the bank. Our savings are just about done."

"We still have *some* money left, don't we?" said Isabella anxiously.

"We have enough to last the summer but not much thereafter," he explained. "The truth is, we'll be out on the street if we don't get our hands on some quality merchandise and *soon*. Perhaps you could get yourself invited to that new girl's house, the one from Zurich. Her father is a banker, I heard."

Isabella shook her head. "I don't know her well enough yet."

"We don't have a lot of time, Isabella," said Nathanial with some urgency. "Living the way we do costs a *great* deal of money, you know that." He sighed again, deflating into the armchair. "If we can't get our hands on some quality merchandise soon we'll just have to go back to Grimethorpe."

"I won't go back," said Isabella firmly, her large eyes clouding over. "No matter what happens, I'll never go back there."

Nathanial leaned over and kissed his daughter's cheek. "Of course not, princess," he promised, though he did not sound very convincing. "Don't worry, we'll figure out something. Now, let's talk of happier things."

"Yes," said Isabella, the darkness lifting from her eyes just as quickly as it had appeared. "I got a letter this morning. It could be just what we are looking for."

"Oh?" Nathanial was only half listening, his attention now largely taken up by a tray of sugar-free toffee fudge. "A letter, you say?"

"Yes," said Isabella with a studied sigh. In fact, Isabella had been saving the letter up until just the right moment to spring it on her unsuspecting father. "It's from someone you might know, actually. Your brother *Silas*."

Nathanial gasped sharply, which sent the toffee hurtling toward the back of his throat. It took several hacking coughs before Nathanial was able to dislodge the toffee fudge and breathe properly again. Sitting back, he took a sip of water, stealing fleeting glances at his daughter.

Isabella offered him a cool smile. "Something I said?"

"Of course not, princess," he said meekly. "You just caught me by surprise, that's all." Nathanial cleared his throat again. "You were saying something about a letter." He coughed, as if choking on the words. "From my brother."

Isabella reached into her pocket and produced the royal blue letter with the thin silver band. She slid it across the top of the bureau toward her father. "I believe it's what you might call an *opportunity*."

Over the next half hour Nathanial read the letter several times; then several more times. His mind began to spin at an increasingly frantic pace as ideas bloomed in his imagination, each one more delicious than the one before. Finally, he beamed at his daughter, barely able to control his joy.

"This is the big one, Isabella!" he declared triumphantly. "My brother is sick, and he wants to meet you; that can only mean one thing—Silas is going to leave everything to *you*." Nathanial's eyes swept across the top of the bureau where the envelope lay. "Err… there was some mention of a check for your expenses."

"It's in a safe place," said Isabella firmly.

"Yes, of course," said Nathanial with little enthusiasm. "Good thinking."

"It's curious that you've never mentioned this brother of yours before," said Isabella, resting her head against the plush cushions. "Does Uncle Silas have money?"

"Oh, yes. He is worth a fortune," said Nathanial.

"What?" Isabella sat bolt upright, the disbelief rippling through her voice. "I've been stealing necklaces and watches from my friends so we can pay the rent and you never thought to mention your brother is a *millionaire?*"

Her father shifted about uncomfortably in his chair, his tanned brow furrowed in a series of uneven lines.

"Well, Isabella," he said carefully, "it's not that simple. Silas disowned the family when he came into his fortune and refused to share a cent of it with the rest of us. Generosity is not in his nature, you see."

Isabella frowned as an unpleasant possibility came to mind.

"Perhaps I wasn't the only one who got a letter from your brother," she said. "You've told me so little about your family. I have cousins, I suppose?"

"Most likely," said her father with a shrug. "My sister Prudence has a daughter I think, and my brother Julius had a son, but I believe he was killed by a volcano."

"A volcano?" Isabella looked horrified.

"I believe so," said Nathanial vaguely. "Wiped out the boy and his parents, as I recall." He sighed, carefully patting down his luxurious head of black hair. "Nasty things, volcanoes."

"How awful. Still, if your sister has a child," Isabella noted, swiftly getting back to business, "I could find myself with some competition for your brother's fortune."

"It's nothing you can't handle, princess. Just remember, my brother is a devil, and he won't be an easy mark."

"Maybe not," she said confidently, "but I believe I'm equal to the challenge. If there's one thing you've taught me, Father, it's how to make a good impression. Give me a few weeks, and he'll love me like his very own daughter."

Her father nodded his approval. "If anyone can do it, you can. For my part, I'll tell you as much as I can about Silas and the rest of the family. This is it, princess. There's a fortune at stake here, and only you can get it for us."

"Relax, Father, I already have a plan of attack," Isabella told him sweetly. "This will be the easiest money we ever made."

Milo

3

"Still fits me like a glove!" said the maestro triumphantly as he admired his impressive reflection in the wall mirror of the dimly lit bedroom he shared with his grandson Milo. "I had this tailcoat made for me in Vienna just before I conducted my first symphony and just look how it fits me still!"

"Amazing," said Milo as he struggled with the astoundingly difficult task of doing up the buttons on the maestro's tailcoat. "Could you breathe in a little more please, Maestro?"

"Breathe in?"

"Your stomach," said Milo. "You need to suck it in...just a little."

"If I breathe in any more I will pass out," declared the maestro, slightly wounded that there was any *sucking in* required of his perfectly flat stomach.

Milo Winterbottom and his grandfather had lived in the tiny basement apartment for two years—ever since the maestro had abandoned his life in Florence and come to Wales to take care of his ten-year-old grandson, after the boy's parents were lost in a tragic accident.

"There, all done," said Milo, wrestling the final button into place.

"Tonight, Milo," announced the maestro grandly, "the Wrinkly Symphony Orchestra will bring beautiful music to the world." He smiled brightly. "Well, at least to the Winslow Square Community Theatre."

The Wrinkly Symphony Orchestra was a ragtag group of retired orchestra musicians whom the maestro had collected during his travels around the city. Their free concerts were a favorite for many residents of the square.

"The curtain rises at eight," said the maestro, adjusting his bow tie. "You will be there, yes?"

"Sure I will," said Milo, brushing down his grandfather's jacket. "I just have to make a delivery for Mrs. Boobank first."

The maestro stopped in front of a three-legged writing table leaning up against the wall; it wobbled perilously as he opened the drawer and removed his baton case.

"You work too hard, my boy," he said somberly.

"I like working," he lied. "Besides, Mrs. Boobank pays me well, and we need the money."

The maestro blew a loud raspberry. "What good is money?"

"Maestro, we cannot *live* without it," said Milo wearily as he cleared the lunch plates off the table and wiped them clean. "If you would just collect *some* of the money your students owe for their music lessons—"

"Bah! You worry too much, my boy."

"Maybe I do," said Milo diplomatically. "But still, we must eat." Picking up his skateboard, he pushed his grandfather toward the front door. "Time to go, Maestro. Winslow Square is waiting!"

And with that, they headed out in the fading light of late afternoon.

ℓℓℓℓ

It must be said that Milo did not look like a typical Winterbottom, although he did have the trademark dark hair that flopped over his forehead in wavy bangs. But while his father had been famous for his dark eyes and brooding good looks, Milo had his mother's complexion—her pale skin, large green eyes, and shy smile.

As they strolled across the main square, the maestro occupied himself with preparation for the forthcoming concert, unaware that Milo's head was filled with more troubling matters concerning the letter he had tucked away in his back pocket. It had arrived in the mail that morning and was sent by his Uncle Silas.

The man who had murdered his parents.

When Milo was nine years old his mother fell gravely ill with pneumonia. Her condition required complete rest, and because they had very little money to pay the doctors, Mr. Winterbottom contacted his brother Silas and asked him for a loan to cover the mounting medical expenses. Milo's father Julius was an honorable man, and he promised to pay Silas back every penny with interest.

Silas refused his brother's plea and told him to go *begging* somewhere else.

But then, rather unexpectedly, Silas Winterbottom had a change of heart. He called his brother with a proposition. Several months earlier Silas had purchased twenty hectares of forest on a peninsula overlooking the Pacific Ocean. The land had been a bargain owing to the fact that it had a dormant volcano deep beneath its rocky surface.

Not bothered by expert predictions that the volcano was several decades overdue for an eruption, Silas went ahead with his plans to build a cluster of luxury villas along the peninsula, which he intended to sell for obscene amounts of money.

Because the land was covered in a blanket of thick pine trees, Silas needed the services of a land clearer before construction on his villas could begin. Unfortunately none of the local clearers would take the job. They feared that disturbing the land over the volcano might trigger an eruption.

Unwilling to abandon the project because of a few cowardly tree cutters, Silas came up with the perfect solution. His idiotic brother Julius was begging him for money—some tedious story about his wife being ill—so why not make the fool earn it? After all, it was a fair exchange; money for labor.

Without delay, Julius was offered the job and as an extra incentive, the use of a small cottage perched on the edge of the peninsula. Naturally, the desperate man jumped at the offer, thrilled that he could bring his family along for the summer.

Silas decided that there was really no need to inform his brother of the volcano lying beneath his new home. After all, it had been dormant for the last one hundred years and there was no point worrying the simpleminded brute unnecessarily.

Barely a week later Milo and his parents found themselves living in paradise. They moved into Evermore, the pretty white cottage overlooking the Pacific, and Julius got to work clearing the pine forest. It was hard, backbreaking work, but he did not mind at all. His family and their happiness was all that mattered.

And they were happy.

Milo spent his days exploring the cliffs and caves near the cottage—which he suspected were inhabited by perfectly approachable dragons—while his mother rested under the warm summer sun, her health slowly mending.

It was a hot day in late August when it happened. Julius had spent the morning leveling a rocky outcrop just inside the forest wall, puncturing the hard rocky crust with a powerful jackhammer. Returning to the cottage at noon, the exhausted man and his wife sat out on the porch eating their sandwiches and enjoying the sea breeze blowing in from the Pacific.

Milo had been called for lunch, but he was too busy peering into a small cave opening set into the cliff's rock face to consider eating. It was at that exact moment—for reasons that are complex, lengthy, and rather dreary—that the surface of the peninsula buckled and split as the volcano, long sleeping, began to wake. The earth trembled, just slightly at first and then with such a deep unease that it made the sides of the cottage shake.

Milo's mother was the first to notice that something was very wrong, but by the time she jumped up and began racing toward her son, it was all too late. In a thunderous chain reaction, the peak of the volcano erupted in a powerful explosion, spewing into the air huge boulders carried on a blast of poisonous gas, followed by a raging torrent of flaming black and orange lava.

When the volcano's first blast shook the peninsula, Milo looked back to see a wall of molten ash looming above him in a great seething wave. Reacting immediately, the young boy jumped from the cliff ledge and swung his nimble body into the small cave below. He heard his mother calling his name just before the second blast exploded from the crater. Frantically he looked overhead for his parents; he thought he heard his father screaming, his body sent hurtling across the peninsula on a wave of sulfuric acid and water vapor, a spinning dot in the distance. Perhaps it was him. And for a brief moment he was certain he caught a glimpse of his mother in her favorite dress—a brilliant flash of blue and white in the far horizon.

And then she was gone.

Cowering against the hot cave wall, Milo could only watch as the last of the molten ash and lava spewed from the volcano's summit, raining over the Pacific like a million heads of fire. It was nearly nightfall when a helicopter descended from the smoky haze to rescue the boy…

His parents' bodies were never recovered. It was assumed that if the lava had not killed them then the ocean most certainly would have—they were probably eaten by sharks somewhere off the coast.

Rather like the volcano, Milo's life erupted that day and never recovered.

Leaving his grandfather at the stage door, Milo raced to Mrs. Boobank's busy florist and began making his afternoon deliveries. He took purple tulips to an irritable-looking woman on Harding Street, three dozen roses to a small house on Kipling Lane, and a bouquet of lilies to a tearful lady with white hair who was retiring after thirty-seven years at the Winslow Square Bank.

Milo then headed at considerable speed for the Winslow Square Community Theatre. By the time he arrived the concert was already well under way so he snuck in through the stage door and watched the remainder of the performance from the wings.

The orchestra was in fine form, a sea of wrinkly faces more glowing and alive with each wave of the maestro's baton. The small crowd listened enthusiastically to the performance, the stage awash in a rich golden light. But the brightest light of all was coming from the maestro as he stood before his beloved orchestra, waving his baton and making beautiful music.

"I don't think I've ever heard Beethoven sound better," declared Milo after the concert. He and the maestro were walking the three short blocks from the theater to the Little Paradiso—a cozy café where they ate once every two months as a special treat. During supper the maestro entertained Milo with a story about his violin lesson with Mrs. Elma Teesdale, who was not the most delicate of players and had a tendency to savagely bash the strings with her bow. Milo laughed loudly, but the maestro could see the faraway look in the boy's eyes.

When their bellies were full they began the short walk home, heading silently across the main square.

"Forgive me, Milo," said the maestro softly, "but I know something is troubling you tonight. Are you feeling unwell, my boy?"

Milo let out a deep breath. He should have known better than to try and keep anything from his grandfather. "I received a letter from my Uncle Silas."

"Mamma mia!" The maestro was stunned to hear that name. "Your mother wrote many years ago and told me all about this *Silas*. Even after he offered your father work, she did not think him to be a good man."

"He is the worst sort of man," said Milo sharply.

"For what reason did he write to you?" asked the maestro.

Milo reached into his back pocket and produced the crested envelope, handing it to his grandfather. They sat down together on the cool stone steps of the town hall while the maestro read the contents carefully. When he was finished he handed it back to Milo without saying a word.

They were just a few blocks from home when the maestro spoke again. "Your uncle has great wealth."

Milo shrugged. "I suppose so."

"His letter," said the maestro with some apprehension, "it could be that he wishes to help you. After all, a dying man can often have a change of heart."

"What are you saying, Maestro?"

"I am saying," said the maestro softly, "that perhaps your uncle can offer you security; money and that sort of thing." He shrugged sadly. "Things I cannot give to you."

"I'd rather eat a dirt sandwich than go anywhere near Silas Winterbottom!" said Milo fiercely. "I'm sorry, Maestro; I know you're only saying this because Silas is rich, but I don't want any of his money! Not his ten thousand dollars; not a single cent!"

The maestro raised his hands in defeat. "As you wish, my boy," he said. "But you know *money* is not the only reason to visit Silas. No, not at all."

The boy scowled. "What do you mean?"

"I mean...maybe there are some things you want to say to him while there is still time. Face-to-face, yes?" He patted Milo on the back. "It might do your heart good to get this anger off your chest."

Milo said nothing, and the subject was not raised again the rest of the way home. When they arrived back at the tiny apartment Milo lit a fire and filled a pot with water—they would have hot chocolate before bed as they did after every meal at Little Paradiso.

While he was waiting for the water to boil, Milo sat by the fireside and pulled the letter from his pocket. He read it once more—each arrogant word a reminder of why he hated his uncle so much—and remembered what the maestro had said about confronting Uncle Silas *face-to-face*. He thought of how cold-bloodedly that heartless villain had sent his parents to their deaths just to satisfy his own greed...and how they were lost to him forever.

He felt a deep satisfaction as he tore apart the check for ten thousand dollars. Yes, such a large amount of money could help them a great deal, but it was poisoned money, and he did not want any part of it.

"See you soon, Uncle Silas," he said coldly, throwing the pieces into the glowing fire. "I'll make you sorry you ever invited me to Sommerset."

The Master of Sommerset

"The master's coming!" shouted Atticus Bingle, his voice echoing down the long vaulted hallway of the servants quarters. "Do hurry up!"

The gilded elevator descended steadily through the entrance hall like an enormous gold and silver birdcage, as a procession of servants and maids scurried across the polished stone floors below, quickly arranging themselves in a perfectly straight line.

They watched as the magnificent cage dropped silently past the upper levels and came to a smooth stop on the ground floor. The ornate doors parted, sliding open like an iron curtain. In the center of the cabin, washed in the reflected glow of the gold and silver bars surrounding him, Silas Winterbottom stared out at his staff with the intense glare of a hungry vulture.

Among even the oldest servants of Sommerset House, the appearance of their master never failed to chill. After all, the sight of a thin, ghostly white man with fierce dark eyes and long black hair sitting regally in a wheelchair with a twelve-foot crocodile at his feet was enough to strike cold fear into even the bravest of souls.

Silas's long bony fingers rested on the chair's joystick that had been cast from liquid bronze into the shape of a crocodile's head; complete with sparkling rubies for eyes and a mouth full of pointed silver teeth.

"Good morning," said Silas soothingly.

"*Good morning, Mr. Winterbottom,*" replied the servants in unison.

Silas pushed the joystick forward and the chair rolled silently out of the elevator cage and into the massive hall. Thorn, the twelve-foot crocodile, lifted his heavy, scaled body from the cage floor and sauntered alongside the moving chair, his long broad snout sweeping from side to side seeking out any sign of danger in the room.

"Tell me," said Silas, "who was the *delightful* maid I heard humming in the hallway outside my bedchamber at exactly six minutes past seven this morning?"

From among the line of servants a solid-looking girl with honey-blond hair and a rather egg-shaped body stepped forward. Her eyes slid down toward the crocodile—Thorn's ancient gaze fixed on her.

"And what is your name?" said Silas sweetly.

"My name is Ursula Vovko," she replied.

"And the music you were humming," said Silas, "what was that?"

"Folk music, Mr. Winterbottom, from Slovenia," said Ursula. "My Grandma Tonka taught me many songs when I was a little girl."

Silas tilted his head slightly, his gaze intense. "Fascinating."

"I hope I didn't disturb you this morning, Mr. Winterbottom," said Ursula, folding and unfolding her arms rather nervously.

"Heavens, *no*," said Silas. "I adore Slovenian music; such a gift to the world. I only regret that ill health prevented me from leaping from my bed and doing the polka."

Ursula giggled, blushing. "I am sure you have heard better voices than mine, sir."

"Perhaps," said Silas brightly. "But yours is so very distinct, possessing all the natural melody of a fire alarm."

A few sniggers rippled along the line of servants.

The chambermaid smiled awkwardly. "Well, thank you..."

"And to show my appreciation for your musical gifts, I have selected you to take Thorn for his morning walk." Silas held out a large metal choker attached to a length of thick chain. "It's the least I can do."

To say that Ursula was not keen on taking the scaled reptile for a walk would be something of an understatement. Ursula's hands shook violently.

"Er...I am not so good with crocodiles," she said, instinctively taking a step back. "You are very kind, sir, but perhaps you might choose someone else?"

"But I choose *you*," said Silas.

"Sir, *please*...I do not think..." Her voice trembled. "I cannot do it."

"Nonsense," said Silas softly. "You can and you shall." Silas shook the leash at her playfully. "Hurry now, Thorn likes to take his walk before it gets too hot."

With tears pooling in her eyes, Ursula took a tentative step toward Thorn and extended her trembling hand to retrieve the leash. As she did Silas tapped his fingers exactly twice on the joystick, the band of his thick gold ring rapping lightly against the brass crocodile head. To the staff assembled in front of him the gesture was meaningless, but to Thorn it was a command, like drumbeats in an ancient forest. The crocodile's wet nostrils seethed and flared and before anyone knew what was happening, Thorn had charged toward Ursula, his large jaws cracking open, unleashing a thunderous growl.

The perfectly formed line of servants broke apart amid blood-curdling screams as maids and kitchen hands rushed frantically to the far reaches of the entrance hall.

Ursula stood frozen—her eyes pierced in terror, her legs locked to the floor as Thorn's gaping jaw rushed at her, his large jagged teeth glistening under the diffused light coming through the glass dome above. With a fierce crack, the beast's jaw snapped shut barely an inch from her outstretched hand—hot breath tickled the fine hairs along her arm. She would have screamed in sheer horror, but her voice, like her body, was frozen in terror.

Calmly Silas tapped his fingers three times on the brass joystick. Instantly Thorn started to back up, his large webbed claws clicking on the stone floor as he retreated. Ursula remained utterly still.

Silas observed the young woman with a fascinated glare. "Remarkable," he said, more to himself than anybody else. "She is *utterly* frozen."

It was true. The fear had caused complete paralysis. The vast entrance hall was rendered silent, as if holding a collective breath.

Very gradually Ursula began to tilt—just slightly at first. Moments later, as if in slow motion, her toes lifted from the floor and she began to fall back, crashing at impressive speed on the stone floor like a block of cement.

The spell was broken and the servants rushed toward her—a group of under-butlers and a few gardeners made several failed attempts to lift Ursula from the floor before Mrs. Hammer had the good sense to call for a stretcher. After some debate about how best to move her, the frozen maid was rolled onto the stretcher and carried into the library, where she remained, her condition unchanged, until the paramedics arrived and took her away.

ℓℓℓℓ

"She'll have to go, Bingle," said Silas, passing through the large conservatory doors leading into the garden. "It's unfortunate, but there you are. The girl is clearly terrified of animals."

"Very well, Mr. Winterbottom," said Bingle dutifully. The soft-spoken butler had worked at Sommerset for more than thirty years and his entire life had been devoted to the service of Silas Winterbottom. His only goal was to make his master happy. "I will see to it."

"By the way," said Silas, "have you made the necessary arrangements for my other *special* guest?"

Bingle nodded, lowering his voice. "Everything has been arranged, sir. All of the supplies were delivered down below as you requested."

"Excellent. Remember, Bingle—it is vital that my friend's presence on the estate remains undetected." Silas smiled thinly. "He is rather eccentric and values his privacy a great deal."

"Of course, sir," Bingle assured him. "Apart from Mrs. Hammer, who will assist me when your guest arrives, no one will know he is here. You have my word, sir."

Outside the morning sun sprayed soft yellow light across the flower beds, each one blooming with a different color rose. The twelve acres of beautifully tended gardens directly behind the conservatory were Silas's private escape—a series of interlocking garden rooms connected via a gallery of imposing iron gates.

Silas maneuvered his chair along the flagstone path between two rows of white and orange roses. Beyond the flower beds was a sunken pond and Thorn lowered himself into the cool water. The pond was filled with salt water and from its position at the far end of the garden provided the ideal swimming hole for the crocodile.

A low groan echoed across the terrace as an ornate iron gate swung open. A solitary figure in dull gray overalls and a large straw hat closed the gate behind him and walked slowly along the garden path.

"The tea roses are not looking well, Moses," said Silas tersely. "What is wrong with them, and what are you doing to fix the problem?"

"Mildew on the leaves," said Moses gruffly. "I'm treating them—should be fine in a week or so."

"I'm glad to hear it," said Silas with considerable relief. "I want to discuss the new seedlings for the west pavilions this afternoon. We will meet in the greenhouse at four, Moses. Do not be late."

Moses grunted, turned his back, and shuffled toward a bed of white roses on the far side of the garden. Silas tilted his frail head back and felt the morning sun slide across his narrow face. It felt like a warm pair of hands.

"Silas, you look well!" said a commanding voice from behind him.

Silas swung his chair around swiftly. "Whitlam, what a wonderful sense of humor you have," he said calmly. "I look like a man on the brink of death, and you know it. Now, what news do you bring for me?"

"Quite a bit, in fact," said the wrinkled little man with the stub nose and the impressive mass of curly white hair. Whitlam had been Silas's attorney for more than forty years, and he was well accustomed to the rather curious demands of his oldest client. Yet even he had been astounded when Silas had suddenly instructed him to locate Adele, Milo, and Isabella Winterbottom for the purpose of inviting them to Sommerset, despite having ignored the children's existence entirely up until that point. He was also deeply moved to see a dying man reaching out to his family after a lifetime of neglect.

"Well," snapped Silas impatiently, "what is it?"

"I have heard from your nieces," Whitlam informed him. "You'll be pleased to learn that they have both accepted your offer. In fact, they seemed positively delighted by the invitation."

Silas nodded knowingly. "That is no great surprise—their parents would gladly walk through fire for a slice of my fortune." He caressed the ring on his finger. "What about the boy?"

"I have spoken with Milo," said Whitlam as he took a seat under the shade of a white pergola.

"Well, what did he say?" said Silas, his dark eyes glistening. "Has he agreed to come?"

"He has."

"Excellent!"

"However," said Whitlam, taking a pair of silver spectacles out of his pocket and cleaning them on his tie, "your nephew has a few conditions."

Silas's right eyebrow arched. *"Conditions?"*

"To begin with, he refuses to accept the ten thousand dollars," explained Whitlam. "He considers it a bribe."

"How remarkable. What else?"

"He will only come to Sommerset for a period of two weeks."

"Two weeks!" hissed Silas. "No, that isn't enough time!" Noticing the queer expression on Whitlam's face, Silas softened his anger. "What I *mean* is—how am I to assess the boy's suitability as my heir in just two weeks?"

"Well, I'm afraid you will have to. The boy's made it perfectly clear that his conditions are not up for negotiation," said Whitlam. "It seems Milo does not wish to be away from his grandfather for any longer than that."

"How touching," said Silas flatly.

From the back of the garden Thorn crept out of the pond and slithered slowly between the flower beds, sinking down onto the warm ground at his master's feet.

Whitlam smiled admiringly. "He's a stubborn boy, that's for sure."

"His father was the same," said Silas coldly. "Stubborn and sentimental."

"Will I tell Milo you accept his conditions?"

"Tell the boy whatever he needs to hear," instructed Silas, the urgency crackling in his voice. "I want Adele, Isabella, and Milo under my roof by the end of the week. I will not surrender to death until I know the future of Sommerset is secure. Whatever it takes, Whitlam—bring the boy to me, and bring him quickly."

The First Arrival

A few days later a grand black limousine with darkened windows, sparkling hubcaps, and a silver crocodile hood ornament collected Ms. Adele Winterbottom from the airport.

Sitting in the backseat, Adele wrestled with a constant stream of fears—about how Silas would treat her, about her cousins and whether they would hate her red hair, about her mother's threat to have her sent away to Ratchet's House.

As the limousine headed deep inside the rain forest, she peered out at the great cathedral of soaring trees, hanging vines, and slick foliage.

"Is this where my uncle lives?" she asked.

The chauffeur laughed warmly. "Not quite, Miss Winterbottom, but we are close. Hold on now, Miss."

Without warning the car veered off from the main road and swung to the left. Ahead of them was a thick wall of green vines twisted and tangled like a wall of knotted ropes. The road curved away from the dense barricade of vines, yet the limousine did not; in fact, the black limousine thundered forward and Adele shut her eyes just seconds before impact.

Then she heard the slapping sound of the long knotted vines sliding over the limousine's roof. Adele opened her eyes—they had passed through the wall of vines and were now on the other side, heading along a sealed road sheltered by a canopy of elm trees.

Ahead, the narrow road tracked between a dazzling display of wet prairies and mangroves surrounded by a thick blanket of willows, vines, and shrubs. As the narrow road came to an end the limousine turned down a small incline and came to a stop in front of a set of ornate iron gates supported by two massive stone posts.

Silently the gates opened and the limousine crossed into a narrow muddy bank on the crest of an enormous swamp covered with lilies and saw grass. In the middle was a large island shielded by a series of mangrove and red maple trees.

"Uncle Silas lives over *there?*" said Adele. She looked searchingly up and down the bank of the swamp. "How do we get across? I can't see a bridge."

"Look," said the chauffeur, pointing to the muddy water directly in front of them.

Adele watched as the surface of the water began to ripple and swirl. Then, without warning, the swamp's surface parted and an enormous white platform began to emerge from below. Adele blinked several times. Whatever was coming to the surface looked like the top of a large rectangular spaceship and stretched from the bank of the swamp to the edge of the island.

A bridge was coming up!

The bridge, underpinned by a series of hydraulic lifts, emerged impressively from under the swamp. Adele had barely got over *that* surprise as she caught a fleeting glimpse of several dark alligators being lifted up out of the water on the bridge. She gasped, pointing at the water with a trembling finger.

"Alligators!" she cried, her voice cracking.

The chauffeur's hearty laugh filled the limousine. "Right you are, Miss," he declared. "The master has dozens of them living in the swamp. He's very fond of reptiles, the master is."

Very quickly the alligators scurried over the edge with a flick of their razorback tails and plunged back into the putrid swamp water. The limousine moved across the bridge and wound its way through rich fields of wildflowers and cultivated lawns that stretched out endlessly on either side of the gravel drive. The beauty of it lifted Adele's mind from the murky depths of the swamp and soothed her; she lowered the window and took in the delicious perfume blowing up off the flower beds. Everywhere she looked there were more gardens—sweeping vistas of brilliant green flaring in the sunlight; open fields teeming with wildflowers, orchids, and rowan trees; majestic waterfalls shooting ribbons of water high into the air; marble statues of rather pompous-looking men and long hedged paths bordered by hawthorn trees covered in dazzling red berries.

They passed through a wide arched gateway and then Adele saw it. *Sommerset House.* It looked more like a castle than a house! Fronted by a long expanse of imposing ribbed vaults, the mansion featured dozens and dozens of full-length windows that swept up into a series of arches like an ancient cathedral. Soaring towers built with massive sandstone blocks loomed along the east and west wings of the house, each many stories high and topped by pointed spires.

As the limousine approached the portico with its thick columns of black marble, a large cloud passed overhead, blocking out the sun. Dark shadows fell across the mansion's façade, swallowing the sharp edges of the stonework. Still gawking at her uncle's grand home, Adele was suddenly struck by the form of the house. For a moment, just a second or two, it began to look monstrous—like a great squatting beast, the spired towers rising up like massive arms, talons poised to strike, the round windows of the central tower, two pulsing gray eyes. A chill rushed at her. She gasped.

Mercifully the clouds shifted and Sommerset House was glorious once more, bathed in a honeycomb sheen.

The limousine came to a gentle stop under the portico, and Adele reminded herself that houses, even ancient ones like Sommerset, did not have claws, and they certainly did not have eyes!

Even so, as a rather brutish-looking butler opened the car door and ushered her through the massive front door with its grand marble arch, her legs would not stop trembling. Once inside, however, there was little time to ponder all that she had seen. A rather lumpish-looking creature was hurrying toward her, barking orders at the maids who trailed after her like a flock of penguins. They all wore long black dresses topped with crisp white aprons and they appeared to nod in unison whenever the wrinkled old lady spoke. Dutifully, they collected Adele's luggage (which consisted of an old suitcase, a parcel of books, and a backpack) and fled up the enormous staircase.

"Welcome to Sommerset House, Miss Adele," said the old woman, revealing a warm smile. "My name is Mrs. Hammer, and I am the head housekeeper. Please follow me."

The young girl followed the bowlegged housekeeper through the massive entrance hall, topped by a soaring glass dome that seemed to reach up into the sky. Her dark eyes sparkled as she passed the gold and silver elevator.

"Uncle Silas has his own *elevator?*"

"Two actually," said Mrs. Hammer. "But the other is just a service elevator and not nearly as grand as this one. Come, we must hurry, your uncle is expecting you."

Mrs. Hammer led Adele down a long corridor flanked by a series of stained-glass panels displaying an array of exotic flowers and plants. They entered a vast reception room full of old-fashioned couches and stiff wingback chairs. Large paintings decorated the walls and all seemed to feature very wrinkly men and women looking entirely miserable. Crossing the room briskly, Mrs. Hammer passed through a number of heavy oak doors that led directly into the Sommerset library.

The young girl spun around with a sense of awe. The library swept up an amazing three stories; the high walls lined in a grid of oak shelves packed to the rafters with books of every conceivable shape and size.

Adele was so caught up in the wonderland of books stacked all around her that it took a few moments for her to hear the sound of someone approaching behind her. Taking a deep breath, she turned, preparing to meet Uncle Silas for the first time.

Her eyes bulged. Then she screamed at the top of her lungs and leaped onto a mahogany reading table.

Thorn dragged his scaly belly along the dark wood floor of the library, his webbed claws clicking furiously across the room. Seeing the strange girl perched up on the reading table made him nervous, and he lunged toward her, his jaw springing open like he was a murderous carnival clown.

Adele let out another piercing scream.

The beast reared his neck up, snapping at the tabletop just inches from her leg. Adele slid across to the far end of the table, her eyes roaming the floor for signs of the scaly monster. Beneath her the creature dropped back to the floor, turned away, and slithered toward the doorway.

Still panting in terror, Adele looked over and saw a sickly looking man with long dark hair sitting in a wheelchair by the door. He was smiling, but Adele could not be certain what sort of smile it was.

"I see you have met Thorn," said Silas, gliding into the library. "You may get down, child."

Adele didn't move. Getting down seemed like a positively stupid idea.

"Is…is it tame?" she asked.

"Certainly not," said Silas, offended by the idea. "He is a savage beast."

"He could eat us all!" she shouted.

"Indeed," said Silas brightly. "Fortunately, Thorn only attacks on command."

"You promise?"

"I do." Silas's face softened slightly. "Come down, Adele, I should like to take a look at you."

With considerable hesitation, Adele climbed down from the reading table and walked slowly across the room toward her uncle. The crocodile showed her no further interest, lying down in front of the fireplace and resting his mammoth jaw on an embroidered cushion.

The closer Adele got to her uncle the more he seemed to resemble a ghost—with his gray skin, flowing black hair, and powdery white eyebrows. Her steps got smaller. He was the strangest looking person she had ever laid eyes on.

"Come closer, child," said Silas softly.

Adele stepped tentatively toward her uncle.

"Closer," whispered Silas eagerly.

Her spine tingled. She took another halting step. For some time Silas's crackling eyes looked her over, from the top of her bright red hair down to her worn sneakers.

"What an interesting looking girl you are," said Silas finally, "and so very *orange*."

Adele bristled at the remark. You see, her hair had always been a sore point. The professor delighted in reminding Adele that the Winterbottom clan was famous for their luxurious *dark* hair. "It is tragic," her mother would declare, looking at Adele's red locks with disdain. "If you weren't my daughter I would swear you were part orangutan!"

"My hair is not pretty," Adele told her uncle matter-of-factly, "but it will not last forever. When I am older I'm going to dye it black."

"I see," said Silas, a sly grin playing on his thin lips. "Well, for what it's worth, I think your hair is quite remarkable. Now tell me, how is my dear sister?"

"The professor—I mean, *Mother* is very well."

"Excellent." Silas grinned. "And tell me, did she send you here to get my money?"

Adele gasped, her face draining to a pasty white. "Uncle Silas, what a terrible thing to say!"

"Nonsense," said Silas sharply. "Your mother is as devious as a caged rat, and I am well aware of your family's desperate financial circumstances."

Adele did not know what to say or where to look. Silas's words cut through her like blades. It was as if he had opened her up and could see everything she was trying to hide.

"I have upset you," said Silas, watching her with a certain fascination.

"No, you haven't," said Adele, biting on her bottom lip.

"I am not angry at you, child," said Silas warmly. "The truth is I admire your mother's greed. So please do not think I judge you harshly. Your mission is a noble one, and I wish you luck."

Silas moved his chair over to the fireplace and pushed a silver button. "You must forgive me, Adele, for I am not well enough to entertain you this afternoon," he said, waving Mrs. Hammer into the library and instructing her to show his niece upstairs to her room. "I shall see you at dinner—six sharp. I prefer to eat alone, but while you are here we can take our meals together."

With that Mrs. Hammer placed her arm on Adele's shoulder and led her out of the library. They walked up a set of back stairs to the third floor and turned into a wide corridor bathed in soft afternoon sunlight. Mrs. Hammer opened the first door on the right and ushered Adele inside a spacious, beautifully furnished room with bright comfortable chairs, a large canopy bed that looked like it could sleep five people comfortably, and a warm fire burning in the hearth.

"It's a fine room," declared Mrs. Hammer. "The master wanted you children to have the best of everything."

Adele nodded, still too upset to speak.

"Well, you get some rest now, Miss Winterbottom, and I'll have one of the maids bring you up a snack in an hour or so."

Mrs. Hammer took another satisfied look around the bedroom chamber before excusing herself. Finally alone, Adele collapsed on the canopy bed. Uncle Silas was a cruel man! Winning his trust and affection seemed an impossible task—he already knew why she was there and what the professor wanted her to do. Feeling the weight of her mission, Adele surrendered to the tears she had been holding back all day. With no one around to hear her in the vast empty wing of Sommerset House, Adele buried her face in a pillow and cried long into the afternoon.

Planting Seeds

It was a raining heavily when Silas, followed loyally by Thorn, made his way into the conservatory to greet his new arrival—Miss Isabella Winterbottom. He found the girl sitting patiently in a large armchair, her hands neatly folded in her lap. She was wearing a pretty white dress and had a silk ribbon around her silky black hair.

"Uncle Silas!" she yelled as the ghostly master of Sommerset moved toward her. "I'm so happy to finally meet you!" She jumped up and embraced her uncle, planting a large kiss on each of his pale cheeks. "I cannot thank you enough for inviting me to Sommerset," she said excitedly. "This is the most beautiful place I have ever seen!"

"I'm glad you like it, Isabella," said Silas. He watched Isabella's face with a sense of delicious anticipation as he waited for the young girl to look past his chair and see the predatory reptile slinking along the floor behind him.

Like clockwork, Isabella's large blue eyes dropped from her uncle's gaze to the ground behind him. Silas leaned closer, waiting for the terrified scream to tear from her lungs.

"Ohhhh, how cute!" she purred, crouching down to pat the creature on the sharp contours of his swampy green flesh. "What is his name, Uncle?"

For once Silas was lost for words. He turned his chair and watched in amazement as Isabella stroked his deadly pet as if it were a puppy. For his part, Thorn growled softly at the strange girl, thoroughly enjoying the attention.

"His name…is Thorn," Silas managed to say. "You are not *afraid* of him?"

"Oh, no," said Isabella, laughing gently. "I think he's sweet."

"Indeed," said Silas, unable to conceal his disappointment.

"Now, Uncle," said Isabella, getting to her feet. "There is one piece of business I would like to get out of the way." She reached into a pocket and produced a folded envelope that she passed to her uncle. "This is the check for ten thousand dollars that you sent to me. I am returning it to you."

"Returning it?" said Silas with not a little indignation.

"That's right," said Isabella matter-of-factly. "The truth is, my father has been very successful in business, and I had no need for your money. It would be a terrible waste if I took money I didn't need, don't you think?"

Silas could only nod. The young lady entranced him as she glided about the conservatory like a princess in her palace. The performance was extraordinary!

"Tell me, Isabella," he said casually, "do I look sick to you?"

"Oh, yes, terribly sick, Uncle," she said earnestly. "In fact, I was just thinking to myself, *poor Uncle Silas is the sickest looking thing I've ever seen.*"

The pale man smiled thinly. "How very honest you are."

"There is one more thing I wish to clear up," said Isabella, who had walked the length of the conservatory and was now touching the dark narrow leaves of a potted fig tree. "I know that you are dying and that you have probably invited me here to decide if I would make a suitable heir." She stopped and looked at her uncle intently. "I'm right, aren't I?"

"Possibly," said Silas.

"Then I need to make one thing very clear, Uncle," said Isabella firmly. "I have no interest in your money or your house—as beautiful as it is. In fact, if you were to make me your heir I would have to refuse." She smiled warmly at Silas. "I hope you're not too angry with me."

Isabella peered closely at her uncle's darkened eyes—they seemed to be dancing. "Not at all," said Silas soothingly. "Such frankness is a very rare thing. How old are you, child?"

"I'm thirteen," said Isabella proudly.

"You are the eldest," he said playfully, leading Isabella through the morning room and into the entrance hall. "I expect you will be a good influence on your cousins."

Isabella stopped suddenly. "Did you say *cousins?*"

"Indeed," said Silas. "Adele and Milo—they are your *cousins*, are they not?"

"Yes, Uncle, but I'm a little confused," said Isabella. "Wasn't Milo Winterbottom killed by a volcano?"

Silas's eyes narrowed, as if he were reaching for a memory that he had long since discarded. Finally, his eyes crackled. "Oh, *that,*" he said grimly. "There was an eruption, that much is true; however, your cousin Milo was not a casualty. It seems he was playing in a cave when the volcano erupted." Silas ran a bony finger over his bottom lip. "Not disappointed, are you?"

"Disappointed?" Isabella cleared her throat—the certainty flooding back into her refined voice. "I'm thrilled! When father told me that poor Milo was dead, I cried for hours. But now I have *two* cousins to get to know. Oh, Uncle, this is the best day of my life!"

"I hope there are even better ones to come," said Silas as he summoned an under-butler. "Escort my niece to her room, and make sure she has everything she needs."

Isabella kissed her uncle and once again declared her unimaginable happiness before following the under-butler up the grand staircase. She gave a final wave to Silas, climbing the large marble stairs with all the poise of a princess in a castle.

Silas watched until she disappeared into the corridor along the eastern wing. After returning to the conservatory, he fed Thorn from a silver tray layered with raw strips of water buffalo, and then summoned Mrs. Hammer, informing the head housekeeper that his niece was to be given every possible attention.

"Of course, sir," said the housekeeper with considerable enthusiasm—Isabella had deeply impressed Mrs. Hammer on their first meeting by complimenting the old lady on her remarkably youthful appearance (which was complete nonsense because everyone who knew Mrs. Hammer agreed that her face resembled a baked potato). Isabella had made particular mention of her *dignified* nose and *delicate* ears. "She seems like such a delightful child!"

"Watch her closely, Mrs. Hammer," instructed Silas. "Watch and listen—I want to know everything she does."

"But, *sir*, surely you don't suspect her of any wrongdoing?"

"She is a Winterbottom," said Silas proudly. "I would expect nothing less."

The Reluctant Guest

Please make yourself comfortable, Master Milo," instructed the bald under-butler with the enormous bottom lip. "Your uncle will be along shortly."

Milo Winterbottom was determined to hate Sommerset from the moment he accepted his uncle's invitation. Yet, as the limousine had crossed the bridge, weaving between acres of gardens exploding with color and meadows teeming with wildflowers, his hatred dissolved into awe and wonder.

For a boy who spent most of his free time in a florist, the grounds of Sommerset were a kind of nirvana. Everywhere he looked thousands of blooms sprang up from among sparkling rivers of lush green lawn in a tapestry of colors.

It was only after the limousine had pulled up outside Sommerset House and Milo was ushered into a walled garden and told to wait that he came back to his senses.

"If you need anything," said the under-butler, "just press the button above the yellow tulips. Someone will come immediately."

Milo smiled stiffly. "Thank you."

The butler bowed dutifully, then disappeared through a black iron gate.

A tide of nerves churned in the pit of Milo's stomach and he suddenly felt terribly alone. He found it impossible to simply sit there on the stone bench and wait for his uncle, so he decided to explore the gardens properly. Perhaps that would take his mind of *where* he was and *who* he was about to meet. Under a large trellis in the center of the patio his attention was immediately drawn to a bed of brilliant blue flowers. He crouched down, looking closely into the eye of the bloom.

"She's a beauty, that one," came a rasping voice from over his shoulder. Milo looked around and saw an old man in muddy overalls, his watery eyes unblinking and rather mischievous. "I'll bet me cotton socks you don't know the name of that rose you're admiring."

Milo took the challenge, studying the flower intently. "Well, from the shape of the head it looks like a Myriam rose...but I've never seen one this color before."

"Course not, but you're close. This here is a hybrid, created especially for Sommerset." He nodded briskly. "By the way, name's Moses."

Milo stood up, feeling rather proud of himself. "Nice to meet you Moses—I'm Milo. Have you worked at Sommerset for a long time?"

"Too long," he muttered, and then pointed to the flower beds on either side of the trellis. "What about this lot then?"

"Leanders," said Milo confidently. "And those over by the far wall are Prominents and then Caesars and Montanas."

The old gardener grunted in approval. "Tell you what, there's a special rose I reckon you'd like to see—it's called the Phoenix rose, and the only place she grows is here at Sommerset." He scratched at his gray whiskers and a troubled look came over his face. "They're hidden away, of course. The master don't like to share 'em with anyone."

"Why not?" asked Milo.

"Because they are precious," said another voice, its melodious tones sliding into Milo's eardrums like trickles of icy water. "But for *you* perhaps I can make an exception."

The boy spun around.

"Hello, Milo, I am your Uncle Silas."

Milo didn't reply. He just stared at the ghostly figure sitting before him, his uncle's long rakish fingers drumming upon the velvet armrests of the antique wheelchair. The frailty of the gaunt, gray face and withered body shocked the boy, but it was Silas's thick dark hair and the glimmer in his jet-black eyes that hit Milo like a punch to the stomach. They were just like his father's. And yet, he detected none of the warmth and laughter that rippled through his father's ebony eyes. Instead, Milo found two dark pits staring back at him—empty and bottomless.

The next thing Milo noticed was the massive crocodile passing along the forecourt. He blinked several times, quite convinced he was having some sort of hallucination.

Silas laughed softly. "That is Thorn. Don't worry, he is perfectly tame...most of the time." Silas then turned his attention to Moses.

"I want you to go and supervise the gardeners working down by the great lake. Last time those fools pruned my rosebushes it looked as if they'd used a meat ax. Hurry along."

Without saying a word, the gardener shuffled off toward the passageway.

"He is half demented, the poor man," said Silas casually. "Not to mention half blind. I should dismiss him, of course, but it's not in my nature to be ruthless."

"He seemed very sane to me," said Milo, crossing his arms.

"Yes, well, looks can be deceiving," said Silas lightly. "Perhaps you would like to see more of the garden?"

"No, thank you," said Milo shortly.

After a few moments of painful silence, Silas escorted Milo through a corridor of gates leading to the main house. It was Milo who stopped as they passed under the last stone archway. He didn't look at Silas. Deep inside the boy, at the very center of his being, a call was being made. Milo knew that if he did not answer it he would regret it for the rest of his life.

It's now or never, he told himself.

"Is there something wrong, Milo?" said Silas.

Milo cleared his throat. "I don't like you, Uncle Silas," he said softly. "I know that's not a nice thing to say, especially to someone who's dying—but it's just how I feel. Well, I just thought you should know."

"I admire your honesty," said Silas calmly. "My only request is that you judge me not by reputation, but rather, by your own observation.

Milo, you know my time is very limited." He watched his nephew closely. "I hope you will try and understand how very much I want to get to know you and your cousins." Silas smiled softly. "So please, Milo, can you show even a little mercy to a sick old man?"

"How much *mercy* did you show my parents?"

Passing by his uncle, Milo walked toward the house without a backward glance.

"Don't just stand there, you lazy girl, get in here and *help* me!"

Standing in the middle of her elegant bedroom suite, Isabella eyed the maid with considerable fury. After all, she had been left to unpack her luggage without assistance. Not only that, the cup of chilled lemon water and the slice of freshly baked sourdough she ordered had not arrived.

"And where are my refreshments?" she demanded to know as the rather timid-looking girl entered the bedroom.

"Refreshments?"

"My lemon water!" she snapped. "My sourdough!"

Kneeling down in front of a large circle of matching luggage, Isabella unzipped one of the bigger cases and threw it open. "Nothing is where it should be!" she roared. "I told Svanhildur to pack all of my formal clothes in *this* bag, but, of course, she has not. What an unprofessional dwarf she is!"

Isabella buried her head in the suitcase, thrusting her hands deep into the stack of neatly packed clothes and then stopped, glaring up at the servant girl.

"Why are you just standing there?" she hissed.

"Well, um, you see—I'm Adele," said the girl faintly. "I saw you arriving from the window and—"

"How wonderful for you," said Isabella curtly. "Don't take this the wrong way, *Adele*, but Sommerset House has dozens of maids, and I cannot be expected to remember everyone's name. I shall just call you *girl* and you shall call me *Miss Isabella*, is that clear?"

Adele laughed nervously. "I'm not a maid," she said. "I'm Adele Fester-Winterbottom, your *cousin*."

With remarkable speed Isabella jumped to her feet, smoothed down her dress, tightened the ribbon holding her hair in place, and lunged at her newly discovered cousin, wrapping her arms around Adele and squeezing her with all the enthusiasm of a professional wrestler.

"Oh, cousin, it is so wonderful to finally meet you!" she gushed loudly.

"Yes..." gasped Adele, who was finding it somewhat difficult to breathe. "It's nice to meet you too, Isabella."

Releasing her grip, Isabella stood back and took a good look at her cousin—what a sad-looking creature! She would be *no* competition at all.

"I already feel like we are sisters, don't you?" said Isabella. "Not that we look alike, of course—you are so pale and then there is your hair." She reached out and felt the frizzy tips of Adele's flaming red hair. "Oh, you poor thing!" she said mournfully. "Are you teased *awfully* at school?"

Adele felt the blood rush to her freckled cheeks. She wanted to melt into the floor and disappear. "No," she mumbled. "In fact, some of my friends really *like* my hair…"

"Oh, you are funny, cousin," said Isabella, laughing. "Now tell me, have you met our uncle yet?"

Adele nodded her head.

"Isn't he the sweetest man you have ever met in your life?"

"You think Uncle Silas is *sweet?*"

"Oh, yes," declared Isabella. "He could not have been kinder to me—he is so warm and cuddly…and Thorn is just the cutest little crocodile I ever saw!" She smiled at Adele. "Don't you agree, cousin?"

"Well…I guess," she said somewhat doubtfully.

"But enough about dear Uncle Silas," said Isabella, clapping her hands. "Tell me all about yourself, and do not leave anything out. I want to know *everything* about you!"

Adele looked at her cousin, in her pretty dress with her perfect skin and silky hair and her polished manners—she would never be able to win over Uncle Silas against someone that perfect. It was stupid to even try.

"There's not much to tell," said Adele meekly. "I'm very boring, really."

"Oh, I am sure there is a lot to tell," said Isabella gazing wide-eyed at her cousin. "I already know about that awful business with your mother and those killer birds. She sounds completely insane!" She smiled at her cousin, failing to notice the humiliation on Adele's face. "What about your father—what is he like?"

"He is very kind," said Adele softly. "He restores damaged books and he has been teaching me—"

"How *interesting!*" interrupted Isabella. "Now, what do you know of our *other* cousin—Milo Winterbottom?"

Adele did not get the chance to answer, because Fremantle, a very tall servant with a tiny head, entered the bedroom carrying a gleaming silver tray. With great care he placed the tray on a side table next to the young ladies.

"I hope the snack is to your satisfaction," he said in a slow flat drawl.

"So do I," snapped Isabella, lunging at the sourdough like she had not eaten in weeks. "That will be all, servant."

Before Fremantle could gather his tray and leave, a frantic-looking chambermaid by the name of Hannah Spoon hurried into the bedroom carrying a set of hand towels and stood nervously in front of Isabella.

"They have been warmed just like you asked, Miss."

"Let me feel them," she mumbled, her cheeks bloated with bread. "That's much better. You may put them in the bathroom, and then you can unpack my cases and place my clothes in the closet in alphabetical order according to color."

"Yes, Miss Winterbottom."

"Oh, and you with the funny head," said Isabella, snapping her fingers at Fremantle. "You may help her with the unpacking."

Before Fremantle had a chance to object, Isabella had grabbed Adele by the hand and disappeared down the lengthy corridor of the eastern wing.

In a cloistered piazza at the western end of the garden, Silas and Thorn moved along a path lined with Sweet Brier roses. Thorn lifted his head and emitted a low growl as Moses passed them, shuffling across the patio, carrying a cardboard box full of potted tulip bulbs.

"How are the Phoenix roses?" said Silas. "Have they opened yet?"

"Nearly open," muttered Moses, not stopping to address his master formally.

"Wait," said Silas firmly.

Moses stopped in his tracks.

"I'm sure I don't have to remind you," said Silas, moving along the path toward the old gardener, "that I do not want any trouble while my nephew and nieces are here."

"I don't make trouble," said Moses gruffly.

"Indeed," said Silas. "Just make sure you don't." He pulled up in front of Moses, turning his chair sharply to face him. "After all, I haven't much time left, and a great deal depends on this visit. By the way, how is your boy Ezra doing at St. Bernadette's—I trust the nurses are taking excellent care of him?"

The old gardener's body stiffened as if the words were a spell that had cast him in granite.

Silas smiled coolly. "Are we clear, Moses?"

A long minute ticked over before Moses finally grunted, indicating that he understood. He then shuffled quickly across the terrace, disappearing into the greenhouse.

Under One Roof

Isabella and Adele passed through the vaulted French doors and entered the sun-filled morning room, sitting down by the large windows.

"It's a beautiful room, isn't it?" said Isabella, leaning back in the chair and sighing deeply. "I don't suppose you have ever been in a house as grand as Sommerset?"

Adele shook her head. "I didn't know they *made* houses this big."

"Oh, cousin!" said Isabella brightly. "Compared to some of my friends in London this house is *small.* My friend Gilda Gettysburg's house in Kent is three times the size of Sommerset."

Adele looked uncertainly at her cousin.

"Do you…do you have a lot of money, Isabella?" she said shyly.

"What a thing to ask!" declared Isabella, but she laughed and looked rather delighted by the question. Then the smile vanished and she was suddenly very serious. "But you have asked and I will answer. Yes, it is true, my father has a great deal of money. It is like I was telling Uncle Silas, I have more money than I know what to do with."

Adele gasped. "You told him that?"

"Oh, yes, cousin. It was obvious he invited us here to pick an heir," said Isabella matter-of-factly, "and I told him that I had no interest in Sommerset. The only reason I have come here is to visit my sick uncle and to meet you and poor little Milo."

A small bud of hope began to spring up inside Adele. Perhaps she did have a chance of winning Silas's favor—especially if Isabella wasn't in the race.

Leaning over, Isabella patted her cousin tenderly on the arm. "You are hoping that Uncle Silas will pick you—am I right, cousin?" Seeing the shocked expression on Adele's face, she smiled. "It's all right, cousin, you can trust me. We are family, after all."

For reasons she could not fully understand, Adele found herself nodding, surrendering to the warmth and understanding in Isabella's radiant blue eyes.

"That's why I'm here," she said softly. "The truth is, my mother wants—"

Adele stopped, the shame overwhelming her. How could she share the horrible truth about the professor's threats with someone like Isabella, whose life was so perfect? Adele was certain that in her cousin's world, mothers were not vile creatures who would throw their children away if they failed to please them.

"Yes, Adele, go on. What about your mother?"

Adele cleared her throat. "My mother…tries her best, but we are always in debt. If we had even a *little* of Uncle Silas's money, it would make our lives so much easier." Her eyes dropped down to the floor. "So much happier."

"Of course it would," said Isabella with certainty. "And I will tell you the truth, cousin—I do not believe Uncle Silas could find a more deserving heir than you."

"Really?" Great waves of relief washed through Adele.

"Of course I do! In fact, I will do anything I can to help you in your quest," she promised, kissing her cousin on the cheek. "In fact, I am going to make it my mission to see that you become the next mistress of Sommerset." She smiled. "You just leave it to me."

"There you are, girls!" said Mrs. Hammer, puffing madly in the doorway. "I've been looking all over the house for you two. There's someone I'd like you to meet." The housekeeper turned around, giving a wave. "Come on now, they won't bite."

From behind Mrs. Hammer's broad black skirt Milo emerged, sliding sideways into the morning room like a crab.

"This is Milo Winterbottom," announced Mrs. Hammer grandly.

In a single move Isabella jumped to her feet and rushed toward the boy, hugging him violently.

"It is wonderful to meet you, Milo!" she declared loudly. "I have prayed for you often over the years, cousin. Oh, it breaks my heart to think how horrible your life has been, you poor little creature. All alone in the world!"

"I am not alone," Milo corrected her, his face still squashed into her shoulder. "I have my grandfather."

"Well, of course you do!" said Isabella, releasing her cousin. She stood back, beaming at him madly. "You are a short little thing, aren't you? Well, never mind that, none of us is perfect."

Adele gave Milo a reassuring smile.

"I'm Adele," she said softly. "Nice to meet you, Milo."

"Nice to meet you," said Milo, shaking her hand.

"The three of us are going to have such fun, Milo," continued Isabella. "Just you wait—this will be the most wonderful adventure we ever had!"

"I'm sure it will," agreed Milo. But he didn't believe it for a second.

Dr. Capon fastened the latch on his medical bag and sat down next to his patient.

"The news is not good," he said gently. "The illness is progressing faster than I anticipated. Your heart is very weak."

Silas opened his eyes slowly and offered the doctor a thin smile. "Indeed," he said faintly. "How long do I have?"

"That's hard to say," said the doctor stiffly. "If you get plenty of rest and take care not to excite yourself...well, who knows?"

"The *truth*, Doctor."

"A month. Less, perhaps."

"I see."

"You must not give up, Silas; people in your condition have been known to live far longer than it was ever thought possible."

"Tell me, Doctor—do you believe in life after death?"

"Oh, well...yes, I suppose I do," answered the doctor, shifting in his chair rather awkwardly. "Not that one can ever know for sure, of course. It's all a matter of faith, as they say." He looked at Silas curiously. "Do you, Silas?"

For a moment he did not answer, and the doctor thought that perhaps his patient had not heard him. Then Silas's pallid lips parted and a small laugh escaped.

"I'm counting on it, Doctor," he said faintly. "I'm counting on it."

"Yes, well, let's not dwell on all that," said the doctor, hastily getting to his feet. "I shall come and see you tomorrow, and I will expect to hear that you have been getting plenty of rest. Is that understood?"

"There is no time to rest," Silas told him, lifting his head from the pillow and reaching for the telephone. "I have a great deal to do and precious little time in which to do it. Your services will no longer be required. Good day, Doctor."

The Uninvited Guest

In the cool shade of an elm tree Silas's face began to glow a golden red as the damp rag scrubbed vigorously across his forehead. Jeremiah Knox, a tall pimply boy with short brown hair, dipped the rag into the polish and continued to buff his master's head.

"You've missed my nose, Knox," said Silas with considerable irritation. "It's right there in the middle of my face, and you missed it."

"Sorry, sir," said Knox anxiously. "I'll do it now, sir."

"Good," snapped Silas, moving his chair toward the large bronze statue that towered over rows of vibrant yellow roses. Following closely, Thorn crawled slowly along the stone path. He growled softly as Bingle raced past wearing an anxious frown.

"Sir, I'm sorry to bother you," said Bingle, bobbing up and down beside the master. "But there's a lady, sir. She's just come across the bridge—she says she knows you."

Silas stared at Bingle, his left eyebrow arching high above a piercing dark eye. The butler took a step back and tried not to look terrified. He gulped. The master did not like unexpected guests. *Ever.*

"It seems, sir," said Bingle softly, his throat suddenly very dry, "that the lady managed to talk her way onto the island. I have called the guardhouse and demanded an explanation and now I shall call security—"

Bingle was unable to finish his sentence because a hot, crushing pain was racking through his body. Silas had moved his chair forward, rolling the front wheel directly over Bingle's right foot. He stopped, the wheel sinking farther into the butler's polished black shoe. The bones in his foot made tight crunching sounds under the intense weight, sending horrific currents of pain shooting up Bingle's legs.

"Sir…my *foot*," he spat through clenched teeth.

"Whoever is on duty at the guardhouse is fired," said Silas calmly. "Immediately."

Just when Bingle thought he could bear the pain no longer, Silas pushed the crocodile-head joystick forward and the chair began to move. Bingle fell to the ground groping at his damaged foot as Silas rolled out of the garden room, followed closely by Thorn.

Emerging from the eastern gate, Silas maneuvered his chair quickly along a path, weaving between Japanese red maple trees and thick clusters of blooming tiger lilies.

Stopping at the edge of the path he looked down the long expanse of drive leading up from the bridge. His eyesight, like his body, was weak, and he squinted, just making out an indistinguishable blob crisscrossing wildly about the road.

With a single tap of Silas's ring, Thorn hunched up on all fours, growling deeply. "Get ready, old friend," said Silas softly. "It seems we have an intruder."

Thorn's large claws scraped over the black tar as he moved carefully onto the sealed road. His nostrils flared as a rush of fury electrified his reptilian senses. The beast let out a furious growl and took off toward his target.

Silas followed, his blurred vision correcting itself gradually as the deranged intruder got nearer. He was rather surprised to see a ridiculous-looking woman with curly red hair, bulging cheeks, and the most unsightly set of teeth he had ever seen riding a worn-out old bicycle up *his* driveway! He recognized her instantly.

Rosemary Winterbottom. His sister.

Completely undeterred by the approaching crocodile, Rosemary began waving at Silas and shouting out, "Yoo-hoo! Hello there, stranger!"

"Haven't I suffered *enough*?" muttered Silas darkly to himself.

Realizing it would not look good if he allowed Thorn to tear apart his own sister, he reluctantly tapped twice on the joystick and Thorn dropped low to the ground and began his retreat. The beast let out a disappointed snarl and swung his spiky tail around, sending several loose stones flying across the road.

Rosemary managed a reasonably dignified dismount from her bicycle before running over and planting a wet kiss on her brother's forehead. She cupped his face, smiling warmly. "Hello, Silas."

His frail appearance caught her off guard and she winced at the sight of his translucent skin, thin as tissue paper; his sunken cheeks webbed with tiny red veins.

"Hello, Rosemary," he said curtly. "It has been a long time."

"A lifetime," declared Rosemary with a rich laugh. She spun around, her coat billowing like a parachute. "What an amazing home you have! All those impressive statues around the place—and every single one of *you!*" She laughed loudly and clapped her hands. "It's absolutely hilarious!"

"I'm glad it amuses you," said Silas, smiling dimly.

"What an enormous lizard!" Rosemary bent down, studying Thorn with genuine fascination. "You always did love those scaly creatures as a boy."

"It is a crocodile," said Silas with just a hint of irritation in his voice. "A *deadly* crocodile."

Rosemary laughed heartily. "How are you, Silas?"

"I am dying, Rosemary."

She nodded. "I heard. I am sorry."

"It is what it is," he said casually, looking over the vast meadows. "But my time is not up just yet, and I intend to use it well."

"That's the spirit!" said Rosemary, her enormous rubbery cheeks bulging and glowing like two red toffee apples. "Don't waste a second, I say."

"Indeed," said Silas doubtfully. He turned his chair and headed back along the path toward the meadow. "It was good of you to come and see me, sister. You know the way out."

"The way out?" Rosemary roared with laughter. "Silas, I'm not going anywhere. You're my brother, and despite the fact that you've ignored my letters for the last thirty years, I love you, and I've come to look after you."

"What a touching offer," said Silas, turning his chair around. "Touching and utterly absurd. I have a dedicated medical team seeing to my every need. Really, sister, you would only be in the way. I must insist that you leave."

"Horse poop!" snapped Rosemary. "I'm staying, and that's that."

"If it's money you want," said Silas coolly, "then you are wasting your time."

"Money?" Rosemary screwed up her nose. "Can't stand the stuff! Turns perfectly fine people into greedy, self-centered nincompoops." She smiled at her brother, flashing two rows of magnificent horse teeth. "I've had a long journey, Silas, and my bones are tired—so stop arguing and invite me in. I'm a stubborn old girl, and you *know* I won't quit."

His black eyes crackled and his lips parted...but only the soft sigh of defeat came out. "As you wish," he said, turning back toward the path. "I will send one of the servants down for your bags."

"No need," remarked Rosemary, untying the string and throwing her frail leather bag over her shoulder. "I travel light."

"Yes," said Silas, with a certain admiration in his voice, "you always did, as I recall."

"It's such a beautiful day," said Adele brightly, "that we thought you might like to see more of the grounds. We could show you the stables if you like."

Milo was peering out from behind his partially open bedroom door. His cousins had not laid eyes on the boy since that first meeting in the library. In fact, he had barely said a single word to either of them, and Isabella had already decided he was not to be trusted.

"He is up to no good, cousin," she declared with certainty. "I just know it."

So it was hardly surprisingly that when Adele suggested they invite Milo for a walk around the grounds, Isabella hated the idea. She claimed it would be a waste of time, as Milo was too short to see over the hedges. But Adele insisted that it was the right thing to do. In truth, she felt sorry for Milo and wanted to make him feel welcome—even if he *was* her main rival for Uncle Silas's fortune.

"So, would you like to come with us?" she asked.

Milo shook his head. "No, thank you."

"Well, maybe you'd like to see the orchard," Adele suggested next. "There's a huge swimming pool nearby with fountains and everything." She smiled warmly at her new cousin. "I know how strange it feels on your first day here. Everything's so new…and big. Isabella and I just want to make you feel welcome." She nudged Isabella in the shoulder. "Don't we?"

"Ouch!" shrieked Isabella, grabbing her arm like she had just been shot. "That hurt! Please remember, Adele, I wasn't blessed with the thick arms of a lumberjack like you—I'm very delicate."

She beamed girlishly at Milo. "But, of course, we want you to feel right at home."

"Don't take this the wrong way," Milo said, clearing his throat nervously, "but it would be better if you just pretended I wasn't here."

"Pretend you're not here?" said Adele curiously.

"That's right. You see, I didn't come to Sommerset to make friends, so there's really no point in us getting to know each other."

"Oh." Adele blushed, her freckled cheeks burning at Milo's rebuff. "Oh, I see."

"I'm sorry," said Milo, immediately wishing he'd kept his mouth shut. "I don't mean to be rude...honestly. I just think it's better this way."

"What an ungrateful little orphan you are!" declared Isabella crossly. "We go out of our way to be nice and this is the thanks we get."

Milo did not know what to say. He'd never been called an *ungrateful orphan* before.

"It's just—" he stammered. "I'd rather stay here if you don't mind."

"It's okay, Milo," said Adele diplomatically. "Really, it's no big deal."

"I know what's going on here!" announced Isabella, wagging her finger at Milo. "Beware, cousin, this boy is utterly devious! He wants us out of the way so he can have Uncle Silas all to himself."

"I do not!" said Milo.

"Oh, yes, you do!" accused Isabella. "Just because you're poor and your parents are dead, you think Uncle Silas will take pity on you and leave his entire fortune to you."

"Isabella!" said Adele. She was stunned by her cousin's cruel accusation.

"That's not true!" said Milo firmly, his cheeks glowing with anger. "I don't want Uncle Silas's money. I don't want anything from him!" He shook his head, his eyes narrowed to dark slits. "You don't know what you're talking about, Isabella."

"Then tell me, Milo," she said, stepping toward the half open door and looking intently at the young boy, "if you didn't come to meet your long-lost cousins and you *say* you're not after Uncle Silas's fortune—why exactly are you here?"

"Revenge," Milo answered softly. "I came here for revenge."

Deep under Sommerset House the master moved easily through the complex grid of tunnels, the tires of his chair cutting across the wet floor, spinning ribbons of water into the air. He came to a stop in a small circular chamber surrounded by the gaping mouths of a dozen darkened tunnels, each one offering passage to places unknown. Just beyond the chamber was a single gray door; a bright light illuminated from around the edges and Silas waited silently as Bingle squeezed past him and produced a large set of keys from his pocket.

Bingle hated trawling the dim tunnels (the cold, rank air of the underground gave him the creeps), but unfortunately he was the only member of the household staff Silas would permit down below. The head butler turned the lock, opening the door.

"As you can see, sir," said Bingle, stepping inside, "all of the deliveries were secured in here just as you instructed."

"You have done very well, Bingle," said Silas. "Everything is ready for tonight's arrival?"

"Yes, sir. Do not worry about a thing."

The brightly lit room was packed to bursting point with a dazzling array of curious supplies and equipment. Dozens of thick glass plates were stacked along the back wall surrounded by a vast selection of electrical tools and machinery. Large crates spilling over with packing straw sat in the middle of the room along with miles of thick cable wire and computer terminals still in their boxes.

At the master's insistence, Bingle had not peered inside any of the crates when they were first delivered. However, as he pushed one of the larger crates aside to make room for Silas, he couldn't help but notice a pair of sphinx statues cushioned among the packing straw. They were breathtaking, covered in hundreds of red and orange gemstones. Unable to resist, Bingle reached in and picked one up.

The precious object felt heavy in his hands.

"Put that down, you fool!" hissed Silas.

The fury in his master's voice struck Bingle with the sting of a lash. His hands shook and before he could stop it, the sphinx had slipped away and plunged to the ground, breaking into several pieces. Trembling now and gasping for breath (for he was certain that Silas would have his head for this) Bingle crouched down to retrieve the shattered sphinx. It was then that he saw the metal cylinder lying among the wreckage. It was approximately ten inches long and half as wide and had clearly come from inside the statue.

As he reached out to pick it up, his eyes fell upon the label printed across the top in thick red lettering: *Plutonium-239*. Instantly Bingle stumbled back, jabbing his finger at the crate.

"Sir, there's plu—plutonium in there!"

"And a large quantity of uranium," said Silas calmly, ignoring his butler's distress. "Absurdly hard to acquire and very costly, but I am told you cannot operate a nuclear generator without them."

"I do beg your pardon, sir," said Bingle as his throat dried up, disappearing in a cough. "Did you say *nuclear* generator?"

Silas nodded slowly.

"But, sir, the whole place will blow sky-high!"

"Don't be so dramatic, Bingle; it's all perfectly safe in the right hands." Silas looked around the room, his dark eyes rippling with pride. "You see, my *special* guest will be undertaking a little building project down here. Something rather extraordinary, in fact."

Despite his curiosity, Bingle knew better than to ask anything further. In truth, he did not really want to know what the master was planning. When it came to the Silas Winterbottom, Bingle learned long ago that some things were better left unsaid.

"Excuse me, sir, will you be dining with the children tonight?" asked Bingle, hoping a change of subject might prompt Silas to leave the basement and return to the safety of the world above. "I know that Miss Isabella was hoping that you would."

"Then I shall not disappoint her."

"Shall we go up then, sir?" said Bingle anxiously. "It is getting rather late."

Silas waved his hand. "You go, Bingle; I wish to stay a while longer."

Before the master could change his mind, Bingle excused himself and walked rapidly back into the maze of tunnels bound for the surface.

Alone and nestled in a welcomed silence, Silas released a satisfied sigh. Everything was coming together as planned. The knowledge that Adele, Isabella, and Milo were finally in his grasp electrified his frail body.

He closed his eyes, spinning dark dreams of Sommerset's next heir.

The Truth

10

The boy is a dangerous lunatic," said Isabella. "He should be locked up!"

Adele frowned. "I don't think he likes us very much. But then, you did call him devious."

"Well, he *is* devious!" snapped Isabella. "You don't really believe he has no interest in Uncle Silas's fortune, do you? Milo is here for the money, I am sure of it. Do not forget, cousin, he is an orphan, and they are cunning little beasts."

"Well...I suppose so."

The setting sun cast a soft light the color of ripe peaches into the large windows of the Sommerset library. Up on the second floor behind a large stack of leather-bound encyclopedias, Adele's frizzy red hair bobbed up and down like the top of a pineapple. She closed her eyes and breathed in the thick odor coming from the musty pages—it smelled like vanilla beans and mothballs.

"This is the most wonderful library in the whole world, isn't it?" she said dreamily. "If it were mine I would throw open the doors so everyone could come and see it." She looked around the soaring cathedral of books. "And I would invite children who haven't enough money to buy their own books and they could come and enjoy the library any time they wanted to."

"What a wonderful idea," said Isabella, who was resting her head against Thorn's back as the great beast slept before the library's grand marble fireplace. "Poor children are my favorite!"

She sat up suddenly.

"Cousin, you simply must tell Uncle Silas of your plans," she instructed. "Tell him about all of those precious poor children you would bring to the island."

"Isabella, I don't know if I can," said Adele anxiously. Just the thought of approaching her uncle made her feel ill. "Uncle Silas will think I am mad if I start telling him what I would do with Sommerset if it were mine. Either that or he will hate me for being arrogant and too sure of myself."

"Arrogant—*you?* Never! Don't forget, dear; Uncle Silas admires ambition and confidence. You have a vision for Sommerset and what a wonderful vision it is! Trust me, cousin, you simply must do it! With Milo scheming to win our uncle's fortune for himself, we have to do whatever it takes to gain the upper hand…for you."

"Do you really think I should?"

"On my life I do, cousin! Uncle Silas will see you are a girl of vision and progress. In short, the perfect heir for Sommerset!"

"All right," said Adele shyly. "I'll try." A smile spread across Adele's face. Her stomach tingled. With Isabella's help, Sommerset was going to be hers!

Just at that moment a thunderous whooping sound echoed through the vaulted library. It seemed to be coming from the hallway outside and both girls looked toward the double doors just as a beaming woman with rosy cheeks and the hair of a circus clown burst through, hooting and hollering.

"Hello, pets!" she bellowed, digging a half-eaten cookie from her pocket and shoving it into her gaping mouth. "Oh, what darling girls you are!"

"Cousin, there's a madwoman in the house!" cried Isabella, trying desperately to wake Thorn from his nap so he could attack the intruder. "Call security!"

"An intruder?" Rosemary laughed raucously. "Heavens, no! I'm your long-lost Aunt Rosemary. Now come over here and give me a kiss!"

The girls were speechless and bug-eyed. Adele was the first to move, walking carefully down the spiral staircase to the library's ground floor. As she crossed the room toward her aunt, Adele was struck by the joy slashing about all over her face and the brilliant red hair on her head. The professor had never spoken much about her sister Rosemary, apart from calling her a *fat spinster* who had *wasted* her life *traveling the world like a bag lady!*

"What a beauty you are!" Rosemary cried, swallowing Adele up in her embrace and planting a cookie-coated kiss on her cheek. She looked admiringly at Adele's hair, her mouth blooming in a gigantic grin. "Magnificent! Isn't red hair a joy?"

"Well...I suppose," said Adele rather meekly.

"Oh, hair can be such a dull business," declared Aunt Rosemary, "all those blondes and brunettes clogging up the streets. But *red*—now that's a color people notice!" She giggled, tapping her niece's freckled nose. "Wonderful! Wonderful!"

Blushing furiously, Adele found it rather difficult to speak. The thought that someone might actually be *glad* to have red hair was utterly shocking. After all, her mother considered Adele's hair a great tragedy, a curse. And it was...*wasn't* it? Even asking the question was bold and new, and the girl's stomach began to tingle.

"And as for *you*," declared Rosemary, turning her attention to Isabella (who was utterly appalled by the pear-shaped, red-cheeked, bucktoothed creature stalking toward her). "Well, you're every bit as pretty as your father described in his letters. And what marvelous eyes! I don't think I've ever seen a prettier shade of blue."

"Well," said Isabella, offering her aunt a faint smile, "that is very kind of you to say, Aunt Rosemary. And your eyes are very...black."

"It's a Winterbottom curse, I'm afraid!" said Rosemary with a grin as she slipped off her coat and threw it carelessly over a chair. She hugged Isabella, planting a wet kiss on her pretty cheek and stunning the poor girl into silence. "Heavens, you remind me of your father! He was a beautiful-looking child, our Nathanial."

Isabella managed a proud smile even as she wiped the slobber from her face. "Our baby pictures are practically identical."

"You've never seen a boy more in love with himself than your father." Rosemary let out a roar of laughter. "And so short! I had dolls taller than he was!"

The girl's smile fell away, replaced by a tense glare. "Come now, Aunt," said Isabella, trying to sound lighthearted. "I am sure you're exaggerating. Father wasn't all that vain, surely?"

"Oh, yes," said Rosemary, dropping down onto the couch and letting out a lengthy sigh. "Nathanial was the vainest child who ever lived. Just ask your Uncle Silas." She giggled again. "His favorite toy was the mirror. The silly boy would spend hours at a time staring into his own reflection. It was love at first sight, our mother use to say." As quickly as she sat down, Rosemary jumped up again. "I must keep moving! I want to introduce myself to your cousin Milo and then have a nap before dinner. I'm dead on my feet!"

With that she grabbed her coat and swept from the library, twirling around when she got to the door and waving at her nieces using both plump arms.

"Lovely to meet you, pets!"

"Miserable hag!" snapped Isabella, when her aunt was safely out of earshot. She sat down on the rug, leaning back against the sleeping crocodile. "She's just jealous because my father is rich and handsome and she is a fat and ugly with big buckteeth and awful clothes. Did you see those big wooden buttons on her coat? I'm certain she made them herself. Probably carved them with her teeth!"

"I thought she was very nice," said Adele rather shyly.

"Don't be fooled, cousin!" Isabella crossed her legs and flicked her silky hair back over her shoulders. "Aunt Rosemary might act all jolly and fat and nice, but she came here for *one* reason only—the money."

"You think so?" said Adele, looking rather alarmed. The last thing she needed was *more* competition.

"Of course! Think about it—she's been gone for thirty years without a word, and suddenly, just when her rich brother is dying, she pops up again." Isabella nodded with certainty. "Trust me—she wants Sommerset all for herself."

Adele moved closer to her cousin and whispered, "What should we do?"

"I'll think of something," said Isabella firmly. "We've just got to keep our eyes open and make sure Uncle Silas does not get taken in by her cheap tricks."

"I'm glad you are here, Isabella," said Adele, looking rather relieved. "You know so much more about people than I do. I don't think I'd have any chance of getting Sommerset without your help."

"Don't be silly," said Isabella, smiling sweetly. "That's what cousins are for."

Way down in the very depths of her heart, in the small part of Isabella that wasn't a selfish criminal, she felt a stab of guilt for the way she was deceiving her cousin. But what choice did she have? Isabella and her father would be bankrupt within six months if she didn't win over Silas. In fact, she really had no other choice than to string Adele along and then destroy her at just the right moment.

"Now, are we done yet?" Isabella moaned. "We've been in here for *hours*."

"It's only been twenty minutes," said Adele. "Besides, I'd gladly spend all my days roaming these shelves."

Isabella rolled her eyes. "How strange you are, cousin." She lay back, resting her head against Thorn's circular tail.

"And even if I was offered a million dollars I wouldn't part with a single book from these shelves," declared Adele. "Not one."

"Who would *want* them anyway?" said Isabella with a very unladylike snort.

Adele laughed. "Lots of people, silly. My dad knows collectors who spend their whole lives roaming the world looking for books just like this."

"They do?" Isabella sprang up, her blue eyes glistening. "So you're telling me these books are valuable?"

"Oh, yes," said Adele, rather pleased that her cousin was finally taking an interest in the library. She pointed down to the glass cabinets along the far wall. "Some of those in there are priceless."

"How funny," said Isabella with a little giggle. She lay back down and closed her eyes, yawning loudly. "Still, what do I care about a bunch of silly old books?"

"Milo hates you," said Rosemary, picking a piece of roasted duck from her gigantic molars. "I was watching him all through dinner and every time you spoke he'd give you such a *look*—eyes like daggers!" She laughed heartily. "And he's a smart boy, a *good* boy—I can tell. He won't be easily fooled, even by an expert like you, Silas."

Rosemary rested her very ample backside against her brother's mahogany desk and picked up a crystal bowl full of walnuts.

"I have no idea what you're talking about," said Silas, rubbing his temples. It had been a long day and his frail body yearned for sleep. "You always did have an overactive imagination, sister."

"Horse poop!" said Rosemary, crunching loudly on a walnut. "You know *exactly* what I mean. This game you're playing—choosing an heir from among three children you know nothing about; it's doomed to failure."

Putting the bowl aside, Rosemary passed through the open French doors and stepped out into the oval courtyard, bathed in the pearly glow of a half-moon. Silas joined her, his cold bones welcoming the warm evening breeze.

"And why do you think it will fail?" said Silas casually.

"Well, for a start, Milo thinks you're the devil himself," said Rosemary. "And Isabella and Adele are only after your fortune—and why wouldn't they be? You've been dangling it in front of them like a prize at a carnival. Instead of looking for the best in the children, you're encouraging the greed in them."

"Sister, I have no interest in who is the most *worthy*," Silas told her calmly. "My estate will go to the one I deem most suitable. Whether they are honest or kind is of no consequence."

Rosemary laughed heartily. "Silas, you're as nutty as a fruitcake!"

"How dare you!" hissed Silas (he was particularly sensitive to any suggestion that he was insane). "I assure you, dear sister, I am perfectly sane."

Plucking a sunflower, Rosemary sniffed it deeply. "We Winterbottoms come from a long line of complete lunatics, Silas, and you know it."

Ignoring the accusation (mostly because it was true), Silas headed toward a large set of grand iron gates. "Come," he snapped, "I want to show you one of my favorite gardens."

"Now? Silas, it's very late."

"The flowers only open at night," he said, the wheelchair moving swiftly down the path. "Come along, sister, the night is fading fast...and so am I."

Rosemary chuckled sadly. She slid the sunflower into a buttonhole on her dress and followed her brother into the fragrant darkness.

Pale moonlight filtered through the frosted arched windows bathing the wide corridor in a blue fog. At the far end of a long hall, a figure appeared from the darkness and moved quickly along the corridor. Glancing back as she went, Adele's anxious face glowed a steely blue. She crossed through two sets of doors before entering a much narrower passageway that curved around the perimeter of the eastern tower.

She had been coming this way since her second night at Sommerset House. It was Mrs. Hammer who had told her about the secret chamber at the back of the library that allowed access to the magnificent cathedral of books without having to pass through any of the main rooms.

Adele's late-night visits to the library were the jewel in her day. She would spend hours alone, going from shelf to shelf, touching the spines of ancient texts, stopping when a particular book grabbed her attention and diving into its pages. A deep peace would fill her and all the worries and anxieties about her mission at Sommerset would fall away.

Coming to the end of the passage, Adele entered a small anteroom linked to an ordinary-looking broom closet. She stepped inside, closing the door behind her and glanced down at her feet.

ONLY IN DARKNESS WILL YOU SEE THE LIGHT.

The words were engraved into a worn slab of white marble at the threshold to the library's hidden door. Mrs. Hammer had explained that the inscription was the work of Theodore Epstein Bloom, the eccentric millionaire who had built Sommerset all those years ago. "He was a spy apparently," Mrs. Hammer told her. "Quite insane, they say. Legend has it that Theodore stumbled across a number of writings that he believed were a threat to mankind. That's why he built this place—to hide the secrets. It was he who carved this message, but he died soon after and no one ever understood what it meant."

Adele's spine tingled as she pushed on the back wall and it began to open. She stopped. There were voices—no more than a whisper—coming from the opposite corridor.

Stepping back, she slipped out of the broom closet.

"Hurry, Bingle, we must be quick!" It was Mrs. Hammer's voice, she was sure of it.

"Shhhh!" hissed Bingle.

Hidden by shadows, Adele crept toward the vestibule linking both passageways. Carefully, she crossed the anteroom, hugging the wall as a faint glow from the gardens fell across her face. Uneasily, she craned her neck around the corner and peeked down the narrow corridor.

It was difficult to see at first, but gradually the darkened figures took shape and she clearly made out Mrs. Hammer pacing nervously back and forth. Then she saw the unmistakable figure of Bingle, limping on one foot. He was accompanied by a third person. A short, bulky figure draped in a long black robe.

The cloaked figure wore a wide hood that made it impossible for Adele to see who or what it was. Holding an arm each, Mrs. Hammer and Bingle guided the figure along the passage, stopping in front of a small door about halfway along the hall.

Suddenly Mrs. Hammer turned, peering down the corridor. Adele held her breath. It felt as if Mrs. Hammer was looking right into her eyes.

"Did you hear something?" whispered the old housekeeper.

Following her gaze, Bingle squinted into the darkness.

"Hear what?" said Bingle curtly. "There's no one there. Come, we must *hurry*."

Hastily, Bingle opened the door and together he and Mrs. Hammer led the mystery guest inside, shutting the door behind them.

A minute ticked slowly by before Adele began to move again. She slinked down the corridor on tiptoes and pressed her ear against the door. Carefully she began to turn the handle—it creaked and twisted like a rusty hinge. She stopped. Hurried footsteps pounded toward her. Releasing the handle, Adele ran back down the corridor. She stumbled, her slippers skidding under the polished floors and fell heavily against the wall. She hid in the darkness—heart pounding.

Mrs. Hammer and Bingle emerged into the corridor looking rather relieved. They exchanged glances, nodding solemnly to each other like they were sealing a secret pact, before walking briskly back toward the servants' quarters.

Adele let out a sharp breath and stepped out of the shadows. Moments later she was opening the door. Inside she found a rather dull-looking storeroom filled with rows of neatly stacked supplies—large boxes with labels like *Third-Floor Light Fittings* and *Silverware Polish*. She crossed into a small alcove filled with pots and pans stacked on makeshift shelves and hanging from the ceiling on large metal racks. Long shadows loomed against the walls and ceiling. There was no sign of the cloaked stranger. Where had it gone? The rooms had no windows and there was only one door leading in and out. She stood there for a few moments, listening intently. Quiet as a graveyard.

"I told you there wasn't anyone around!" snapped Bingle as he thrust open the storeroom door again and hobbled in.

Adele slid under a narrow table in the corner.

"I know what I heard," said Mrs. Hammer anxiously. "Footsteps, that's what!"

The old housekeeper entered the alcove sweeping her eyes over the floor like there was a mouse on the loose. "I was sure I heard footsteps." But there was less certainty in her voice. "I really did."

"It was just your imagination," said Bingle impatiently. "Do let's go, Mrs. Hammer. I need to rest this foot. The pain is unbearable."

"This whole thing feels *wrong*, Bingle," said the housekeeper gravely.

"We are doing what we are told, Mrs. Hammer. Right and wrong have no part to play."

Adele waited until the footsteps had trailed away, listening for the sound of the storeroom door clicking shut before she emerged from hiding. When she was certain Mrs. Hammer and Bingle were truly gone, she ran out of the storeroom and charged down the long corridor, cold fear thumping in her heart. Someone was being hidden in Sommerset House; that much she was certain of. And even though the sight of the cloaked stranger had terrified her, she was determined to find out exactly who it was.

Secrets

Milo spent his first few days at Sommerset snooping around the island trying to learn more about his mysterious uncle—but had little luck. It was as if everybody who worked for Silas Winterbottom was too terrified of the sick old man to say one word against him. Milo was starting to fear that his mission was doomed to failure.

It was as if his uncle's shadow loomed above the entire island like a thundercloud.

Wiping a trickle of sweat from the back of his neck, Milo headed up a set of stone steps covered by an arbor of velvety green leaves, which led up to the orchard. At the far end of the grove, Moses was throwing a net over the branches of a large orange tree. Milo waved to him. The old man saw him but did not respond. Instead he tied a length of cord around the trunk, fixing the net firmly in place, and shuffled off in the opposite direction.

"Don't take it personally," came a voice from above.

Milo looked up just in time to see a gangly teenager leap from a nearby tree.

"He's like that with everyone," the boy remarked, sliding a pair of pruning sheers into his overalls. "I'm Knox, by the way. Jeremiah Knox."

"Hi, I'm Milo."

"I know who you are," said Knox with a smirk.

Milo smiled awkwardly, shuffling his feet across the dirt.

"So," Milo said finally, "I guess you work for Moses?"

"I work for Mr. Winterbottom," Knox corrected him. "Moses is just a crazy old man. The truth is, it's me who runs the gardens here at Sommerset."

"But you're just a boy," said Milo doubtfully.

Knox flashed him a foul look. "I'm old enough," he muttered.

Burying his hands deep in his overalls, the young gardener appeared set to stalk off when he turned and said, "He and the master hate each other, you know?"

"Who, Moses?" said Milo. Finally someone was willing to talk about Uncle Silas!

"That's right," said the teenager slyly. "His boy was in the car with Lady Bloom when it crashed."

"Lady *who?*" said Milo, looking rather puzzled.

"Lady Bloom—she's the one the master was all set to marry," said Knox, relishing the fact that he clearly knew more about Silas Winterbottom than his own nephew. "It was her family that built Sommerset; they lived here for over a century. When Lady Bloom died she left the whole thing to your uncle."

"You said there was a car crash?"

"Happened about fifty years ago," said Knox, pulling an orange from the branch above his head. "Lady Bloom was driving out in the forest, going real fast, they say. Something happened and she lost control of the car. Ran right into a tree. Dead."

"And Moses's son—what happened to him?"

"He was hurt real bad." Knox drove his thumb into the top of the orange and began to peel it. "His brain ain't right, if you know what I mean. The old man still goes to visit him in the nursing home. I tried to ask him about the accident once, and he nearly bit my head off." He lowered his voice to a whisper. "They say Moses knows all your uncle's secrets."

From the opposite end of the field a rather ill-sounding bell began to ring. Milo looked down the grove just as Rosemary rode out from behind a lemon tree, pedaling furiously in their direction.

"What kind of secrets?" said Milo, wanting desperately to find out what the young gardener knew. He turned toward Knox only to discover that he had vanished without a trace.

"Enter."

When Mrs. Hammer opened the thick oak door of the master's study she was wearing an enormous apron covered in baking powder and a very disapproving scowl.

"What is it, Mrs. Hammer?" said Silas sharply, not looking up from his desk. "I am escorting my nieces to the stables this afternoon, so do be brief."

"Sir," said Mrs. Hammer, clearing her throat, "Milo's grandfather just phoned asking to speak with the boy."

"Again?" snapped Silas.

"Yes, sir, and earlier today Adele's father made several calls of his own."

"Don't these fools have anything better to do with their time?" seethed Silas.

"Sir, I must tell you that I am finding it very difficult making up these excuses every time one of them calls," explained Mrs. Hammer briskly. "Perhaps if you just allowed the children to talk—"

"No," hissed Silas. "The children will be told nothing of these calls, is that clear?"

"Perfectly clear," said Mrs. Hammer, unable to hide her disapproval. "But, sir, it's only natural that the children's families are anxious to talk with them. Milo's grandfather sounded so sad on the phone—he's missing the boy terribly." Silas stared at her darkly and Mrs. Hammer felt her resolve wilting. "What I mean is…"

"Mrs. Hammer, the children have only just arrived at Sommerset," explained Silas, his calm manner resurfacing. "I fear that talking with their parents so soon will be unsettling. I am just thinking of the children, you understand? Now, if there are any further calls for the young Winterbottoms, put them through to me directly."

"As you wish," said Mrs. Hammer dutifully.

Feeling rather defeated, she excused herself and retreated to the relative warmth of the kitchen. When she was gone Silas picked up the telephone on his desk.

"Bingle, come to my office at once," he instructed. "I have a job for you."

Rosemary Winterbottom was as stubborn as she was hefty, and so, once she got it in her head that Milo wasn't spending nearly enough time with Adele and Isabella, the poor boy really had no say in the matter. Milo had hoped to spend the afternoon tracking down Knox to ask him more about Uncle Silas, but instead he was forced by his aunt to visit the Sommerset stables for some quality time with his cousins.

Milo's mood wasn't improved when he found Adele, Isabella, *and* Uncle Silas watching a majestic black gelding being put through its paces.

Silas stared intently at the boy as he reluctantly took his place beside his cousins.

"I'm glad you came, Milo," said Silas warmly. "I have seen so little of you since you arrived."

Milo did not reply. Something about Silas's penetrating stare seemed to take the wind right out of him.

"Oh, I adore horses!" declared Isabella, who was wearing a pale pink riding outfit and clasping an enormous riding crop. "Father says I am a natural rider. Do you ride much, Adele?"

"Not really," said Adele softly. "I mean, I've never actually ridden a horse."

"Never?" said Isabella. "But surely you are joking, cousin?" Adele

began to glow redder than a freshly polished apple. In a painfully unconvincing display of regret, Isabella covered her mouth in horror. "Oh, I am such an idiot! Here I am talking about horse riding when, of course, you could *never* afford such an activity! Do forgive me, cousin."

"It's okay," said Adele shyly.

"There's something I need to tell you, Isabella," said Milo somberly, giving Adele a mischievous grin that she did not really understand. "It's something I've been hiding for years, but I just can't live with the shame any longer."

"Well, whatever it is, cousin, you can tell me," said Isabella, rather delighted by Milo's sudden urge to confess a scandalous secret.

Milo cleared his throat and declared loudly, "My name is Milo Winterbottom, and I've never ridden a horse either! Take pity on a poor horseless boy, Miss Isabella!"

Adele and Rosemary began to laugh. Isabella did not. She turned on her heels and stalked toward the stables, followed closely by Hannah Spoon (who was now acting as Isabella's personal maid and was forced to accompany the silly girl wherever she went). As the giggling died down the others headed off in the same direction.

"Well done, Milo," said Silas, moving in front of Milo to block his way. "You managed to prick your cousin's considerable ego with ease. I am impressed."

"I didn't do it for you, Uncle Silas," said Milo shortly.

"No, you did it for Adele. It was a very kind gesture."

"Well...thank you," said Milo awkwardly. Feeling his uncle's intense gaze, he stepped around Silas's chair and caught up with the others as they headed into the stables.

Once inside all three young Winterbottoms were astounded by the incredible number of Arabian horses in Silas's massive complex—each muscular animal dazzled them, their coats shining like silken armor in shades of chestnut, gray, black, and roan. Isabella quickly spotted a stunning black Arabian in a stall at the end of the barn.

"That is the horse I want to ride," she told the stable manager, pointing with her riding crop. "Saddle it up for me at once."

"That's Iris," said Flick, the stocky young stable manager. "She's not ready for riding yet, Miss."

"Why not?" Isabella demanded to know.

"Iris hasn't been broken in yet," explained Flick. "She's a stubborn one, Miss."

"Not broken?" said Silas, coming up behind them.

"Not quite yet, sir," said Flick nervously, "but we are very close."

Silas looked into the open stall where the proud animal was walking in a small circle.

"It won't do," he said. "I have been patient, but I will not stable a horse that cannot be broken."

"But, sir, she's so close," said Flick anxiously. "If we sell her now, she'll end up as a workhorse, and that's no life for an Arabian."

"Get rid of it," said Silas with an icy gaze.

"That's not fair," said Milo angrily. "In just a few weeks she'll be good for riding. It would be cruel to sell her into a life of hard labor all for the sake of a few lousy weeks."

"Yes, it would," said Rosemary, falling in beside her nephew. "*Very* cruel indeed!"

The faintest hint of a smile curled around Silas's dry lips. "Perhaps you are right, Milo," he said. "My poor health is affecting my sense of fairness, it would seem." He turned toward the stable manager. "Flick, put the horse in one of the outer fields—I want you to work on her every day until she has been properly broken in. Is that clear?"

"Yes, sir," said Flick, unable to hide his relief. "Thank you, Mr. Winterbottom!"

"You do have a heart after all," said Rosemary, patting Silas on the shoulder. "What a shock!"

While Flick prepared three medium-sized horses for the children to ride, Milo drifted off to the side of the barn and watched his uncle. The frail man sat perfectly still in his chair, his head held high. Who is Silas Winterbottom *really?* he wondered.

When the horses were ready, the children headed outside. Near the entrance to the stables, Isabella stopped dead in her tracks in front of a large pile of horse manure. She called for Hannah Spoon.

"Do clear away this revolting mess, dear," she instructed with a wave of her crop. "I find stepping over horse manure very upsetting."

Hannah stared down at the manure with a look of considerable confusion. She had never been asked to remove horse poop before and was not completely sure how to go about it. She usually cleared away an unwanted mess with a vacuum cleaner, but that hardly seemed appropriate.

"How should I do it, Miss?" she asked anxiously.

"Use a shovel, girl!" snapped Isabella. Then, linking arms with Adele, she said, "Oh, cousin, you will love horse riding, I am sure of it! Now, I think it might be better if you took the largest horse—after all, you are so much *bigger* than I am."

Adele suddenly felt like an enormous marshmallow. "I'm sure you know best," she said, trying not to sound at all wounded.

Returning with a shovel, Hannah carefully scooped several large pieces of manure from the stable floor and began to look around for a suitable place to throw it.

Isabella stared impatiently at the maid. "Hurry up, dear!" she snapped, bringing her riding crop down onto a wooden post for added effect. As the crop struck the post, a loud crack echoed around the stables that caused a chestnut mare in the adjacent stall to buck, kicking suddenly at the stall door, which flew open. Screaming, Hannah jumped back, which caused the disk-shaped pile of horse poop to fling off the shovel and spin through the air, landing smack-bang in the middle of Isabella's pretty face.

Silas was the first to notice that his niece had disappeared behind an impressive mountain of soft brown manure. Gasping in horror, Hannah Spoon's eyes rolled back in her head and she dropped to the floor like a stone.

"Ahhhhhhhhhh!" Isabella shrieked, scooping away the horse poop covering her eyes. "What *is* this?"

"Horse manure, child," said Silas, his voice melodious.

Isabella released another bloodcurdling scream, which flowed seamlessly into a loud crying fit. She spun around on the spot, causing several blobs of manure to fling off her face. "I'm covered in horse poop!" she cried. "I'm covered in *horse poop!*"

"Indeed," said Silas. He felt his spirits lift on the wings of his niece's distress, and it made him smile. "Well, you *did* say you loved horses, Isabella."

Milo and Rosemary were already laughing their heads off, and Adele, unable to hold it in a second longer, let out the biggest, loudest laugh she had ever produced in her life. It came up from the pit of her stomach and made her whole body shake.

"It's not funny!" shrieked Isabella. She pointed to the unconscious maid on the floor. "She did this to me, the clumsy idiot! I want her flogged!"

"Nonsense," said Rosemary, wiping the tears from her eyes. "It's your fault for banging that silly whip and scaring the horse."

If looks could kill, Rosemary would have dropped dead on the spot from the deadly stare Isabella was giving her. To make matters worse, Milo (whom Isabella regarded as a moneygrubbing little orphan) was grinning from ear to ear, enjoying every second of her humiliation. Unable to laugh anymore because her stomach ached too much, Adele started to feel a pang of guilt over her cousin's humiliation.

"Come on," she said gently, taking her cousin by the arm. "Let's go back to the house and get you washed up."

Isabella nodded faintly and allowed her cousin to pull her along.

"Wait," instructed Silas. "Rosemary, you are to hose this child down thoroughly before she returns to the house." He looked down at Hannah Spoon's unconscious body. "And have someone come and remove *that*."

"Hose me down?" cried Isabella. "Uncle, *please*, I don't want to be hosed down!"

But Silas did not stop to debate the matter. He turned his chair and headed back into the stables as Isabella was led outside. Silas could hear the fresh shrieks of his niece as the cold jets from the hose hit her putrid face for the first time. Later, when he was done inspecting his horses, he stopped by Flick's office.

"About that Arabian," he said. "I have changed my mind. Get rid of her today."

"Today?" Flick could hardly believe his ears. "But, sir, I'll need some time to find a place for her."

"Then shoot the animal," said Silas with a wave of his hand. "I don't care how; just remove that horse *today*." His eyes glowed darkly at the stable hand. "I have no use for any creature that will not bend to my will—including you, Gideon Flick."

"All right, Mr. Winterbottom," said Flick, unable to look the ghostly old man in the face. "I'll take care of it."

"Very good. Oh, and, Flick, say nothing of this to the children. They are too young to understand that sometimes in life you have to be cruel to be kind."

As Silas headed out into the warm afternoon sun, his eyes, which had been dull and lifeless, now glowed like hot coals.

I Spy

At dinner that night no mention was made of Isabella's rather smelly encounter. Seated around a mahogany table, which stretched from one end of the grand oval dining room to the other, the Winterbottoms dined on a simple meal of chicken and baked vegetables with priceless eighteenth-century silverware. Silas, seated at the head of the table, hardly touched his food. Instead, he would look out hauntingly at his guests like a scientist studying rats in a laboratory.

A side door swung open and Bingle entered the room. He bent down beside Silas, whispering into his ear.

"How very inconvenient," grumbled Silas before dismissing the head butler and turning his attention back to his guests.

"It seems that the phone lines have been badly damaged," he announced regretfully. "They will be out of service for several days."

"All of them?" said Rosemary.

"Indeed," said Silas, taking a sip of water. "Naturally, I am furious."

"But I was going to call the maestro after dinner," said Milo with a scowl (he was dying to talk with his grandfather and was rather hurt that the great conductor had not phoned him yet to see how he was doing). "What caused the damage?"

"Apparently there was a rather severe electrical storm last night," explained Silas calmly. "Lightning struck a large maple tree just outside the estate and it fell onto the wires, bringing the whole thing down."

"Really?" said Rosemary. "I didn't hear any storm last night."

"Neither did I," echoed Milo.

"Well, I am pleased no one was disturbed," said Silas with a thin smile. "Do not worry, the phones will be repaired soon enough and then you will be free to make as many calls as you wish." Silas wiped the corner of his mouth with a white napkin. "Now tell me—how are you children enjoying each other's company? Are you all getting along?"

"Oh, yes," said Isabella brightly. "We are like old friends!"

Milo looked at her like she was crazy and Adele kept her eyes firmly on her plate. She was still preoccupied with thoughts of the cloaked stranger. Not to mention her quest to win over Uncle Silas—which had not exactly been a huge success so far. Still, she had Isabella on her side, and tonight was to be the first big step in their campaign!

"I'm glad to hear it," said Silas. "I was worried there might be some *competition* among you three."

"Worried?" snorted Rosemary, shoveling a large piece of baked potato into her mouth. "*Hoping* is more like it!"

"Well," said Silas, "a little competition is good for the soul."

"Oh, but, Uncle, don't you see? There *is* no competition," declared Isabella. "After all, I am already very rich and have no interest in your fortune, and Milo hates you with a vengeance."

"Does he indeed?" said Silas dryly.

"Oh, yes, Uncle," confirmed Isabella. "He blames you for that dreadful volcanic eruption that killed his parents. Don't you, Milo?"

The room went very silent as all eyes swept to Milo. He said nothing at first, remaining perfectly still in his chair, and then he began to nod slowly.

"Yes," he said softly. "Yes, I do."

"How very unfortunate," said Silas. "I had hoped we had gotten past all of that."

"If you think about it, Uncle," said Isabella matter-of-factly, "there's really only *one* person you should consider, and that is Adele. After all, she has so many wonderful plans for Sommerset. Isn't that right, cousin?"

"Well…I guess," said Adele timidly, her mouth suddenly very dry. "I mean, yes…yes, I do. Lots of plans."

"How fascinating," said Silas. "Do share some of them with us."

Adele cleared her throat. Her hands were trembling. This was it. Her chance to win over Uncle Silas. She remembered Isabella's instructions and tried to look as confident as she could—which was not very confident at all.

"I think…" she began softly. "I think the grounds at Sommerset are so beautiful that everyone should be able to come and enjoy it. You know, like a park. A place where people could come and relax or explore the gardens or swim in the pools."

Silas stared at her coolly.

"By everyone, am I to assume you mean the *public?*" he sneered, his pale face screwing up as if he had just swallowed an insect.

"Oh, yes," said Isabella, jumping right in. "And that's not all—Adele would open the library to poor children and all sorts of other unfortunates." She beamed. "Isn't it a wonderful idea?"

"It is *not*," said Silas sharply. "Sommerset is a private estate, *not* a playground!"

"Well, I think it's grand," said Rosemary, patting Adele on the hand.

"Me too," said Milo, offering his cousin an encouraging nod.

But it was no use. Adele could see the fury in her uncle's pallid face. He hated her ideas! She looked to Isabella for help, but her cousin seemed preoccupied with her meal and would not meet her desperate gaze.

"I'm sorry, Uncle Silas," said Adele limply. "They were just… silly ideas. They don't mean anything, honestly."

"I do not feel well," said Silas, closing his eyes. "I shall retire to my room."

He moved swiftly out of the dining room, followed quickly by a gaggle of servants, leaving behind a heavy silence broken only by the sound of Rosemary's chewing ferociously on a chicken thigh. And then, as if nothing had happened, Isabella began talking excitedly about the poached pears they were having for dessert.

Fearing that she would burst into tears at any moment, Adele pushed her chair back, preparing to leave. Her napkin fell from her lap. Reaching down to pick it up, she glanced briefly under the table. Something bright flashed in her eyes. She blinked several times. As Isabella chatted away above the table, underneath it she was folding a fork, knife, and what looked like several dessert spoons into a napkin. Perhaps she was going to polish them, Adele told herself. Then Isabella carefully slid the bulky napkin into the pocket of her jacket. Adele could not believe her eyes!

Isabella Winterbottom would not *steal* silverware from her uncle! *Would she?*

It was after midnight when Adele entered the narrow antechamber and stepped into the broom closet. She was still reeling from what she had witnessed at dinner. Isabella had stolen eighteenth-century silverware from the dining room! It did not make sense—after all, Isabella's father was incredibly rich.

Pushing on the back wall of the closet, Adele stepped over the message carved into the stone floor—ONLY IN DARKNESS WILL YOU SEE THE LIGHT—disappearing inside.

A familiar excitement flooded through her every time she passed through the secret passageway and shut the bookcase behind her. She glanced around the towering shelves. Where should she begin her reading tonight?

Glancing lazily at the rows of books, Adele was halfway down the aisle when her heart stopped. She covered her mouth, her face locked in a silent scream. Silas, his body bathed in shards of milky light, was staring at her from the other end of the aisle. She stumbled, falling back.

"Good evening," said Silas softly. "I see you have found the secret entrance."

Unable to speak and with nowhere to run, Adele got to her feet. Up ahead she heard something move, brushing the ground, but the floor was shrouded in darkness, and she could not see what it was. Peering down, she focused on the shadows—there were flecks of light, silvery and wet, moving toward her. A low snarl broke the silence. Thorn! He was creeping toward her in the darkness, like a beast hunting its prey.

Taking a large step back, Adele hit the end of the bookcase and could go no farther.

Thorn let out a deep snarl and she heard his claws clicking on the floor.

He was getting closer.

"Uncle Silas!" she yelled, shutting her eyes. Tremors ripped through her body and almost instinctively she jumped up, wedging her feet into the bookshelves. She began to climb.

Silas tapped his fingers and Thorn fell silent. "Come down," said her uncle slowly. "Thorn feared you were an intruder. My guests do not usually make their entrance through secret passageways."

Adele legs turned to jelly and she fell back to the floor, tears flooding her eyes. "I'm sorry" was all she could think to say.

"There's nothing to be sorry about," declared Silas, moving his chair toward her. "I am not angry with you, child."

Adele looked up and saw that Silas was holding out his hand. "Come," he whispered. "Do not be afraid."

She took his hand and his fingers closed around hers. They felt like icicles.

"That's better," said Silas warmly. "You see, there is no need to be frightened."

"At dinner tonight," said Adele, her voice shaking, "you were so angry with me."

"Nonsense, child. I was tired, that is all. I may not agree with some of your *ideas*, but I admire your sense of vision." He licked his thin lips. "I know how much this library means to you."

Adele nodded eagerly.

"And one day very soon it could be yours." He watched the young girl's face and saw the idea take hold, filling her imagination and making her heart race. "You would like that, wouldn't you, Adele?"

"Very much, Uncle Silas."

"And you understand how important it is that the next owner of Sommerset possesses the necessary *qualities* to watch over it as I have?"

"Yes, of course," said Adele, trying hard to control the mounting excitement.

"Good," said Silas crisply. "Then you will have no problem collecting a little intelligence for me."

"Intelligence?"

"It is simple really; you will watch your cousins closely—I want to know what they think, what they say, and what they do—especially Milo."

Adele's mouth fell open. "You want me to spy on them?"

"That's exactly what I want you to do."

"No, I couldn't," said Adele, shaking her head. "I can't spy on my own cousins!"

"Should you agree to my request I would be most grateful. In fact, it would show me how serious you were about owning Sommerset one day."

"But, Uncle..." Tears welled in Adele's eyes again. "I can't do it," she whispered.

Silas nodded slowly. "I understand," he said gently. "The choice is yours, naturally. I'm just sorry that a girl with your great potential is going to end up in a place like Ratchet's House."

Adele gasped. "What did you say?"

"Ratchet's House," repeated Silas, savoring each word. "That is where you will be sent if you fail to secure my estate, isn't it? They say no one is ever the same once they've been in *that* place." He shook his head, clicking his tongue. "But I am sure you will adapt to a life without freedom...without your father...without your books."

Although she could not find the strength to speak, the bewildered look on her face said it all. How did Silas know about Ratchet's House? *How?*

"I know everything," said Silas softly, as if he had read her mind. "Did you think I would invite you to my home without first doing a little research? Come now, you are a clever girl."

Adele gasped. "You've known about Ratchet's House from the beginning, haven't you?"

"Indeed." Silas smiled thinly. "I have found over the course of my life that the greatest treasure of all is information. You might say I am a *collector*. And because I know why you came here and what you want from me, I understand you very well. That is why I must urge you to give my offer careful thought. Your future could be glorious, Adele, but nothing in this world comes without a price…and you know mine." He leaned forward, the moonlight illuminating his ashen face. "The question is—are you willing to pay for it?"

Feeling a great weight pushing down on her shoulders, Adele needed every ounce of strength she had left to lift her head and look at Silas. She had to win her uncle's trust if she had any hope of winning his estate. It was foolish of her to think she even had a choice.

"All right," she whispered. "I'll be your spy."

"Excellent," said Silas, a brilliant smile sliding across his lips.

Discovery

Dark clouds hung low over Sommerset, and it rained for the next three days. As a result, the children were largely confined to the house, unable to play in the gardens or ride the horses. Milo felt like he was going mad as he walked through the rooms of Sommerset House, longing to be outside so he could continue his investigation into Uncle Silas. Adele spent nearly all of the time bunkered down in the library occupied by her own troubles. And as for Isabella, she busied herself by barking orders at Hannah Spoon and doing just about anything to gain her uncle's approval.

This proved to be difficult as Silas had taken to his bed with a fever and severe chest pains. The slow passing days at Sommerset came to an end one morning when the sun finally broke through the clouds. Isabella and Milo had a quick breakfast before heading outside. Only Adele remained at the breakfast table playing idly with a piece of toast.

Ever since her secret meeting with Silas in the library she had been lost in a fog of confusion. She truly hated herself for agreeing to become her uncle's spy—yet what choice did she have? It was either betraying her cousins or risk being sent to Ratchet's House for the next ten years.

Mrs. Hammer noticed Adele's sullen mood. Putting down a silver tray stacked with breakfast bowls, she pulled up a chair at the breakfast table.

"Is everything all right, Miss Adele?"

Adele looked closely at the housekeeper. She had kind eyes, yet Adele could not get the eerie image of the cloaked figure from her mind. Who was it? And why were Mrs. Hammer and Bingle hiding the stranger away?

"Everything is fine, Mrs. Hammer," said Adele. "Honestly."

Mrs. Hammer smiled, but she did not seem entirely convinced. "Well, if you're sure."

Later, as Adele was leaving the breakfast room, she heard one of the serving maids whisperingly anxiously to Mrs. Hammer. What was so urgent? Adele wondered. She dropped down on one knee, pretending to tie up her shoelaces and heard the maid say something about a set of ivory dessert spoons.

"Oh, mercy!" responded Mrs. Hammer, clutching her chest. "Are you sure they're gone—have you looked *everywhere?*"

"We have, Mrs. Hammer," said the maid anxiously. "And that's not all. Last night after dinner the silverware count was out by five pieces, and this morning one of the butlers reported a set of porcelain figures missing from the music room."

Grabbing the serving maid by the arm, Mrs. Hammer led her away from the door. "Do not repeat a word of this," she whispered.

"If there is a thief working among us, then I intend to find the guilty party before Mr. Winterbottom ever hears a word of it. Is that clear?"

She nodded. "I won't say a word, Mrs. Hammer."

While the two servants hastily cleared the breakfast table, Adele slipped away unnoticed and headed straight for Isabella's bedroom.

Staring into the darkness, her eyes roamed the area under her cousin's bed. Nothing there apart from a few hair ribbons—certainly no sign of silverware or porcelain figures. Adele stood up and looked around the bedroom. She searched high and low and found no trace of the missing items.

Her nerves were tingling madly, and her heart thumped. Spying did not come naturally to Adele, and her hands trembled as she opened a blanket box.

That Isabella was a thief still did not make any sense—yet Adele could not deny that she had witnessed her cousin stealing the silverware. But if that were true, then where was the evidence? On the verge of giving up, Adele went once more to the vast walk-in closet and searched the pockets of Isabella's clothes.

Nothing.

Reaching to close the closet door she spotted one of Isabella's beautiful winter coats on the floor beneath several pairs of boots. Aware that Isabella would probably holler at one of the maids if she found her coat lying on the ground, she bent down and picked it up. A heavy weight inside the coat made a clinking sound as it tumbled out.

Scattered across the closet floor were an array of items—the missing set of ivory spoons, silverware, the porcelain figures from the music room, a gold carriage clock, silver napkin rings, and on and on.

Adele stood there looking rather stupefied—her cousin was a thief, and worse still, she was *good* at it!

Bending down, she gathered all of the objects and bundled them back into the jacket. As she did her hand hit something hard in the left pocket. Looking inside, she found several small leather-bound volumes from the library.

Adele gasped. Instantly she recognized the books. They belonged to the collection of rare volumes stored in the row of glass cabinets on the ground floor. Quickly she recalled how interested her cousin had become when she heard how valuable the library's collection was.

Searching the other pockets, she found books stuffed in every one—each book was a rare first edition and worth a sizable fortune.

A growing anger gripped Adele. Stealing silverware and statues was bad enough, but how dare she steal *books?* Despite her fury and with considerable difficulty, Adele returned the books to the pockets of her cousin's jacket and packed them away into the far corner of the closet.

Closing the door to her cousin's bedroom, Adele set off for the library, where she began to plan exactly how she would expose the thief of Sommerset.

"Ow!" shrieked Isabella, slapping Hannah Spoon's hand away from her long black hair. "You're pulling it!"

"Sorry, Miss," said Hannah, who had the rather thankless task of doing Isabella's hair as the young lady relaxed in a secluded garden of pink and orange roses.

"Well, be careful," snapped Isabella. She sighed, running her fingers through the long silky strands of her hair. "It is not easy having beautiful hair, you know. You are so lucky, dear—your hair is as stiff as a toilet brush, I am sure you don't even need to comb it most of the time. What a relief that must be!"

"Yes, Miss, a *great* relief," Hannah said through clenched teeth.

Milo was crossing the rose garden looking for Moses when he caught sight of his snooty cousin. He was about to escape through a break in the hedge when Isabella began waving at him.

"Hello, Milo," she said sweetly. "I hardly recognized you from so far away; you are so very tiny! Dear cousin, I hope you are not upset with me about what I told Uncle Silas at dinner. I thought it was common knowledge that you hated him."

Clenching his fists into tight balls, Milo fought against a strong impulse to pick up a bucket of fertilizer and dump it onto his cousin's head. Instead he opted to do something which he felt sure would upset her even more.

"Hello, Hannah," he said, smiling warmly at the young maid. "Have you done something different to your hair? You look very pretty today."

Hannah giggled shyly. "Thank you, Master Milo."

Then Milo passed the two girls, ignoring his cousin completely. A stony scowl set into Isabella's face, and she emitted a low grumbling sound.

"Hurry up, girl!" she snapped at Hannah. "And stop smiling. You look like a monkey!"

Feeling rather pleased with himself, Milo headed for the orchard, keeping his eyes peeled for any sign of Moses or Knox.

"Good morning, Milo."

Milo looked up. He flinched seeing the hollow face staring back at him.

"Hello, Uncle Silas."

He noted how frail Silas looked—his cheekbones raised sharply, his skin ashen and lifeless.

"I have been looking for you," said Silas. "There's something I'd like you to see."

"Actually, I'm kind of busy at the moment."

"Whatever it is," said Silas calmly, "I'm sure it can wait. Do follow me."

Reluctantly Milo did as he was told. Crossing the courtyard, they entered a large greenhouse linked by an enclosed path. Silas moved silently through the long steamy room, leading Milo out into a narrow courtyard with a solid metal door at the far end. He produced a large key from his pocket. The key slid into the barrel and turned, and the door opened with a rusty clank.

Inside was a simple garden surrounded by large stone pillars and high walls. Neat rows of flowers with the most enormous blooms Milo had ever seen ran along the sides, curving around a brass sundial in the center.

"You know a great deal about flowers, Milo," said Silas playfully. "Tell me, what do you think these are?"

Never one to shrink from a challenge, Milo took a closer look. They were incredible—a mass of arched purple petals surrounding a luminous orange and yellow bulb, which seemed to float in the middle like a water lantern. Each flower looked radiant and on fire. He smelled the perfume.

"Recognize the scent?" said Silas, smiling.

"Yes," exclaimed Milo, leaning in and taking another deep breath. "It smells like gardenias…*and* lavender. But how?"

"*How* indeed." Silas gave a satisfied grin. "Do you like the combination?"

For a brief moment Milo considered lying. "Yes," he admitted.

"So, what do you think of the Phoenix rose?"

Milo recalled Moses telling him about the mysterious Phoenix rose the day he arrived at Sommerset.

"It's not like any rose I've ever seen," he said.

"Of course not. It was created right here by a leading scientist—an expert in genetic modification. It is one of a kind. Remarkable, don't you think?"

"Remarkable," said Milo, unable to hide his excitement. "Mr. Boobank would go crazy for this. Could I take a cutting?"

Silas laughed. "The Phoenix rose is a private pleasure," he said.

"It is not for public consumption. You see, the roses in this garden will decorate my coffin."

"A flower this special should be shared," said Milo as he wandered down to the far end of the garden. "Seems selfish to keep it all to yourself."

"Well," said Silas, following after his nephew, "as the next heir of Sommerset you may do with them what you wish."

The words did not reach Milo right away, but when they did his face grew pale.

"Who, me?"

Silas nodded. "Indeed. I have given it a great deal of thought and I am going to leave my estate to you, Milo."

"Wait." Milo shook his head. "But I don't want it."

"Ah, but you will in time," said Silas softly. "You see, I know that you would come to care for this place as deeply as I do. Your cousins do not have your soul, child. You know how important it is to protect what you love and keep it from harm. I truly believe that you and the maestro would be very happy here at Sommerset."

An uncomfortable feeling settled on Milo. His uncle's words eased their way inside him and began to make real sense. It was as if Silas were casting a spell over the boy, and he did not like the feeling one little bit.

"If you love Sommerset so much, Uncle Silas," he told him, "then give it to someone who wants it—because I do not."

"Why not?" snapped Silas, his calm manner slipping away. "I am offering you the *world!*"

"Well, I don't want your world!"

"Then you are a fool!"

"You don't get it, do you?" Milo found himself crouching down in front of his uncle, looking deep into his dark eyes. "When my father asked you for help, *begged* you for help—what did you do? You sent us to live on top of a volcano!"

"Milo, you must understand," said Silas defensively. "I was simply trying to be a good brother. Your father needed money and so I offered him a job. If I had known there was even a remote possibility that the volcano would erupt, well, I would never have suggested the idea."

"Liar!" shouted Milo. "You were warned about the volcano! You couldn't get anyone else to clear that land, so you lied to my father, and he believed you because my mother was sick and he was desperate." Milo felt the tears stinging his eyes. "It would have been so easy for you to lend my parents the little amount they needed. Instead, you sent them to their graves."

"Perhaps you are right, Milo," Silas said softly. "What happened on that peninsula, the devastation it wrought, has haunted me. Every day I think of your parents and wish that I had simply given your father the money he needed. The truth is, I have enjoyed great fortune in my life, but I have not shared it."

The admission took Milo by complete surprise. Was Silas actually admitting his guilt?

"Death is coming for me," he told the boy, his head hanging low, "and I am trying to make up for some of the wrong I have done—especially to your parents. Please believe that I never intended any harm to come to them…or to you. I know all about your life, Milo—how much you and your grandfather struggle just to get by."

"We do just fine," said Milo, but the strength seemed to have left his voice.

"Believe it or not, Milo, your father and I were very close at one time, and I know how deeply he cared for his family. What would he want for you—a life of grim despair in Winslow Square or a life of luxury right here at Sommerset?"

Milo did not answer.

"You think that if you accept Sommerset, then you are betraying your father, but that is not true. Your father would want this for you." Silas took a shallow breath. "Well, take some time, and think it over."

He left Milo in the secret garden, surrounded by the rarest flower on earth—the orange and red blooms sparkling in the morning sun like a fire storm.

The Night of Comings and Goings

As the door opened a shard of light cut across the darkened hallway. Isabella popped her head out and looked up and down the corridor. No one around. She stepped out of her room, quiet as a mouse, and moved along the hall.

Winding down the grand staircase Isabella angrily pulled a large cloth bag from beneath her dressing gown. The object of her fury was Milo Winterbottom. How dare he *ignore* her in the garden… and to tell a lumpy creature like Hannah Spoon that she looked *pretty* was practically criminal!

Isabella picked up a small bronze clock from a long table on the first-floor landing and slipped it into the bag. Hadn't she gone out of her way to welcome Milo when he arrived at Sommerset? Of course she had! And hadn't she hugged him dearly and told him how sad it was that his parents had been eaten by sharks? Oh, yes, she had! And didn't she invite the poor orphan to go horse riding with her? Well…no. But she *meant* to, and that was practically the same thing!

Moving stealthily toward the drawing room, Isabella saw a shadow sliding across the far wall. She froze. Someone else was wandering the halls of Sommerset House! She spun around just in time to see a fuzzy red Afro disappear around the corner.

Adele!

A flash of anger gripped Isabella's pretty face. That tomato-haired little brat was up to something! Dropping the bag, Isabella took off after her cousin.

Adele was on the hunt. En route to the library she had spotted Bingle coming down a set of stairs behind the servants' quarters. He was holding the same cloak she had seen draped over the mysterious houseguest a few nights before. She followed Bingle back to the storeroom, where she now had her ear pressed against the door.

She could hear whispering and the shuffling of feet.

Behind her a slick gray shadow inched along the stone floor. From the darkness a hand emerged bathed in pale moonlight. It moved closer toward her—the fingers flexed, coming down softly onto her shoulder.

Adele jumped, her body seizing up. She covered her mouth to trap the scream that threatened to tear out as she spun around.

"Whatever are you *doing*, cousin?" whispered Isabella with a sly grin.

Before Adele could answer, the door handle began to turn. Grabbing her cousin by the arm, Adele jumped, pulling both of them into the tapestry of shadows splashed across the far side of the corridor.

Bingle and Mrs. Hammer stepped out into the hall.

"You are certain no one saw you?" Mrs. Hammer said anxiously.

"I'm positive," replied Bingle, wiping his brow with a blue handkerchief. "I took the back stairs, and Dr. Mangrove was covered by the cloak the whole time. No one saw a thing."

"I still don't understand why Dr. Mangrove has to be hidden away in the basement," said Mrs. Hammer.

Bingle chuckled softly. "The master stores all of his treasures in the basement, Mrs. Hammer, you know that."

"I still don't like it, Bingle," said Mrs. Hammer. "Why the need for all of this secrecy? And what on earth is Dr. Mangrove building down there?"

"The master's affairs are private," said Bingle tersely. "If you are smart you will ask no more questions, Mrs. Hammer. Curiosity can be a dangerous thing."

Mrs. Hammer gulped loudly. "Yes, yes…I'm sure you are right."

"Good. Now are you certain the entrance is sealed?"

"Yes. I checked it twice."

"Then let us go," said Bingle as they hurried down the corridor. "I will collect the good doctor before sunrise."

Alone again, Adele and Isabella stepped out into the dim light.

"I have a bad feeling, Isabella," said Adele softly. "Who is this Dr. Mangrove?"

But Isabella was not listening, her greedy mind busily spinning. Uncle Silas keeps his *treasures* in the basement, that's what Bingle said. She had visions of priceless artworks, royal jewels, and mountains of gold and silver.

Her skin tingled at the possibilities.

"We must find a way down to the basement," said Isabella, opening the storeroom door.

"It's no use," said Adele. "The entrance isn't there. Or if it is, it's so well hidden I cannot find it."

"But, cousin, we have to! There could be a fortune down there!"

Adele frowned at her cousin.

"This isn't about money, Isabella," she said crossly. "Didn't you hear what Mrs. Hammer and Bingle were saying? Uncle Silas is up to something, and this Dr. Mangrove is involved. We have to find out what is going on."

"Well, of course we do!" said Isabella with a flick of her hair. "That…that is exactly what I meant, cousin. Why should I care if Uncle Silas's basement is full of priceless treasures? Stuff and nonsense! The important thing is to discover what is going on down there…and I think the perfect person to do that is *you*." She yawned loudly. "I am exhausted, cousin; I really must go to bed."

"Bed?" Adele was stunned. "How on earth could you think of sleeping *now?*"

"Oh, cousin, the basement will still be there in the morning," said Isabella playfully (actually, she was thinking about the bag full of stolen property she left back in the entrance hall). "Besides, all of this excitement has exhausted me. Good night, cousin."

Alone again, Adele made her way toward the secret entrance. There were thousands of books on the library's towering shelves.

Surely one of them would be of help in her quest. Sommerset House had a basement, and she was going to find a way in.

ℓℓℓℓ

"I trust you were not seen."

"We were careful," said Dr. Mangrove, smiling confidently. The doctor was an odd-looking man—completely bald (with neither eyebrows nor eyelashes), he possessed a round, puffy face, waxy skin, beady eyes, and teeth a putrid shade of yellow.

"Of course you were," said Silas faintly, taking another shallow breath.

Thorn sniffed suspiciously at Dr. Mangrove's shoes, then dropped to the ground beside his master's bed. His belly was full, and the fat little man did not look all that appetizing.

"Your pulse is weak," said the doctor as he held Silas's bony wrist. "I fear the medicine is no longer helping."

"That is why you are here, Mangrove," said Silas, resting his head back on a stack of silk pillows. "I trust everything is going smoothly down below."

"Perfectly," said Dr. Mangrove. "Do not worry about anything."

"Ah, but I *must* worry," said Silas, sounding utterly exhausted. "The road ahead is fraught with danger. There is still so much to do."

"Yes, you are right." Dr. Mangrove rubbed his thick hands together. "But we are so close, I can almost taste it. The choices we make now are critical."

"Indeed."

"Three children and you can only pick one," said Mangrove, smiling grimly. "From what you have told me, each of them has their charms. Deciding who shall *inherit* and who shall go home is a complex matter."

"Not really," said Silas. "I made my choice long ago, but one must always plan for the unexpected, and that is why I invited *three* young Winterbottoms to the island. I don't need to remind you, Mangrove, how very delicate this project is. After all, you have been working toward this day for a lifetime...for *many* lifetimes. We have but a single chance to get it right, and if the chosen one fails me, then we will have two healthy specimens as backup. I have been watching my guests closely. In truth, I have rather enjoyed toying with them; mind games are excellent sport for a dying man. I need to know how they think, how they react, what they feel. In short, I must see into their very souls."

Mangrove was nodding, his eyes brimming with admiration for the sickly old man. "You have thought of everything, old friend."

"Indeed." Silas closed his heavy eyes. "But as for the children *going home*, well, that is simply out of the question."

"Oh?" Dr. Mangrove licked his lips.

"Even the slightest chance of discovery is too great," said Silas with cool certainty. "No, it was clear to me from the very beginning that the remaining children must never leave Sommerset." He sighed gently. "Not alive anyway."

As Silas and Dr. Mangrove continued their meeting in the secrecy of the master's bedroom chamber, outside an ear was pressed to the door taking in every terrifying word. Fear consumed the eavesdropper who dared not make a sound. Discovery would mean certain death. With a racing heart, the figure moved rapidly from the master's bedroom chamber, rushing toward the welcomed darkness of the landing.

A hand slid into the back recesses of a narrow drawer and pulled out an object wrapped tightly in white cloth—it looked like a mummy emerging from its tomb. With great care the object was being unwrapped. Layer after layer unwound until the knife fell onto the table.

Gripping the white handle, the knife was pulled from its sheath—the blade glistened, throwing blinding balls of white light onto the ceiling. A deep sense of satisfaction pulsed through the silent figure standing alone in the bedroom.

The day was coming when Silas Winterbottom would pay for his cruelty.

Soon it would all be over.

Persuasion

15

Isabella never entered a kitchen if she could possibly avoid it. Kitchens were revolting places where pasty-faced servants and potbellied cooks spent their miserable days preparing delicious food for people like her. The only time Isabella made an exception was when she had a complaint, which is why she was standing beside a table covered with freshly baked banana bread, whining loudly about the temperature of her iced tea (which was much too cold for her delicate mouth). It was during this visit to the kitchen that she unexpectedly learned a very useful piece of information—Uncle Silas's beloved crocodile was allergic to chicken meat. *Very* allergic.

Mrs. Hammer was instructing a new kitchen hand and she made a great fuss regarding Thorn's feeding requirements. Under no circumstances was the beast to be fed chicken. Ever.

This gave Isabella a most wonderful idea.

With a fresh glass of room-temperature iced tea in hand, she went in search of Adele and found the glum little redhead curled up with a stack of books in the library looking thoroughly miserable.

"There you are," she said, flopping down next to Adele in front of the gigantic marble fireplace. "So, cousin, have you made any progress finding a way into the basement?"

Adele shook her head. "I am sure there must be something here that would help...a book or a map. But there are so many books to search through—it will take me *years* to check every one."

"Never mind, cousin," said Isabella with a giggle. "You are such a clever little thing—I am sure you will work it out. Now, on to more important matters. I've had the most wonderful idea to help you win over Uncle Silas."

With little enthusiasm Adele closed the book on her lap and picked up another, scrolling through the index. She sighed heavily. "That's nice, Isabella."

Reaching across, Isabella closed the book her cousin was reading.

"Dearest, you still want to be Uncle Silas's heir, don't you?" asked Isabella.

Adele hesitated for a moment. *Did* she still want it? Chasing that prize had led her down a very dark path—scheming, plotting, working as a spy for her uncle. So much had happened lately and her thoughts were a great jumble. The only thing she was certain of was Ratchet's House and how terrified she was of being sent there. Regardless of what Uncle Silas was hiding in the basement, he was still the master of Sommerset, and she *had* to prove herself to him. She simply had to. And as for Isabella—well, while she was almost certainly a book-stealing criminal, Adele had no choice but to trust her.

After all, who else could she turn to for help? Aunt Rosemary would be horrified if she knew why Adele had really come to Sommerset, and while Milo claimed to hate Uncle Silas and want nothing to do with his fortune, how could she be sure? Oh, it was all so confusing! All Adele knew for certain was that without help she would never win over her uncle.

"Yes," she said faintly. "Of course I do. But why do you want to help me so much, Isabella?"

The pretty girl seemed shocked by the question, but her eyes soon took on their usual knowing gleam. "Because you *deserve* this, cousin," she said. "You may not be pretty or quick-witted or even terribly interesting—but you are good and kind. Besides, I couldn't bear to think of Sommerset going to that insane little orphan, and *I* certainly have no need for it." Isabella patted her cousin on the hand. "Come now, cousin, you must show more determination. Uncle Silas will not hand Sommerset to you without a fight. You are going to have to win his heart."

"Because *that* worked so well last time," said Adele, remembering Silas's bitter reaction to her ideas for Sommerset.

"Well, that's why you must do something spectacular this time!" declared Isabella, jumping to her feet. "And my idea will make Uncle Silas think you are the sweetest girl who ever lived!"

"It will?"

"Yes! Who does Uncle Silas love more than anyone else on this island?" asked Isabella.

"That's easy," answered Adele. "Thorn."

"Exactly! And tonight you are going to cook Thorn a special dinner all by yourself. Uncle Silas will see how much you care for the beast, and he will love you for it!"

Adele quickly came to see that her cousin's idea was a clever one. "Yes, it just might work!"

"The only decision you must make," said Isabella with a frown, "is what to cook. The poor thing eats water buffalo every day—perhaps we could think of something different as a special treat." She rubbed her chin. "Mmm, whatever do crocodiles *eat?*"

"I know!" said Adele excitedly. "Chicken. Crocodiles eat chicken—I read it in one of Uncle Silas's reptile books."

Smiling triumphantly, Isabella could hardly believe her luck. Adele had walked right into her trap. Why, she almost felt sorry for her.

"What a brilliant idea, cousin!" said Isabella, clapping her hands. "Just be sure you don't tell anyone what you are planning; they will just try and take the credit for themselves. No, Uncle Silas must know that this meal was all your own doing!"

At dinner that night Silas was in an unusually good mood. His appetite had returned with a vengeance, and he spent much of the meal humming playfully to himself. Isabella, who looked glorious in a pale blue evening dress with her hair piled atop her head like a crown, was forced to wait until Mrs. Hammer was serving dessert before she could strike.

"Mrs. Hammer," said Silas, "see that Thorn is given his evening meal directly."

"There is no need, Uncle," said Isabella, smiling sweetly. "Adele has already done it."

"She has?" said Silas, his dark eyes sliding over to his redheaded niece. "You fed Thorn all by yourself?"

Adele nodded eagerly. "Yes, Uncle. I spent all afternoon preparing a special meal for him."

Uncle Silas seemed rather pleased. "How very kind, child."

Rosemary, shoveling a huge piece of cheesecake into her large mouth, winked in approval, and even Milo looked impressed.

"Adele is a wonderful cook," said Isabella keenly. "She made Thorn a delicious feast of water buffalo and chicken. It looked delicious!"

"Chicken?" said Silas sharply, his white eyebrows arching high across his forehead. "Thorn was given *chicken?*"

"Yes, Uncle," said Adele with a confident smile.

"*Huge* pieces of chicken," Isabella added gleefully.

By now Adele could see the fury sparking in Silas's eyes, his clenched jaw pulsing tightly under translucent skin. He looked murderous.

"Uncle Silas, is everything all right?" said Adele rather meekly, sliding down in her chair.

"No, it is not," hissed Silas. "Thorn is allergic to chicken, you fool! It is poison to him."

"Poison?" Adele's head was spinning. It was too horrible to be true!

Silas moved quickly from the room, disappearing into the ballroom.

He could be heard frantically calling Thorn's name all over the mansion.

But the beast was nowhere to be found. In desperation, Silas ordered a full-scale search of the house and grounds. Adele felt horribly guilty about the whole thing and blamed herself completely—as did her uncle. He refused to speak to her and instructed Mrs. Hammer to keep the "wretched little brat" out of his sight.

With Adele banished to the kitchen, Isabella (who was feeling very pleased with the success of her plan) retired to her room to change outfits while Milo joined in the search. He scoured the ground floor of the mansion from one end to the other. After several long hours, Milo was just about to give up when he went back into the game room for one final check and found Thorn groaning beneath the billiards table.

Milo was shocked by the reptile's unsightly appearance. Thorn was blown up like a helium balloon, his stumpy legs lifted high above the ground, his large eyes swollen shut.

"How are you, boy?" asked Milo, patting the beast softly.

Thorn could only groan, rolling from side to side like a gigantic beach ball.

With the covers pulled up over her head, Adele was hiding from the world. Only her wild red afro was visible, bursting out from under the blanket like a head of broccoli.

"Come now, cousin," said Isabella, trying very hard not to yawn, "you must look on the bright side. Things aren't *that* bad."

"Yes, they are!" cried Adele. "I nearly killed the one thing on earth Uncle Silas cares about! He will *never* forgive me. Never!"

"The vet said Thorn will make a full recovery," reasoned Isabella. "Besides, I am quite sure Uncle Silas will not hold it against you...forever."

"Yes, he will." Adele pulled the blanket from her face and wiped at her eyes. "Oh, Isabella, how did it all go so wrong?"

"Dearest," said Isabella mournfully, "you must try and stay positive. In the morning things will not seem so awful. And even if Uncle Silas doesn't forgive you, well, at least you have the love and affection of your dear parents. Nothing can change that." She kissed Adele on the cheek. "Nothing at all."

Long into the night Adele lay awake wondering how on earth she would survive in Ratchet's House. For that was certainly her future now. The professor would never forgive her for coming home empty-handed. She would be locked away from her father and her books...from everything she loved.

Later still, exhausted and afraid, Adele sat on the end of her bed and thought back over all that had happened since she first arrived on the island. And as she did, a rather interesting thing began to happen—the events of the past week bloomed like a garden springing up from the earth; things she had seen, things she had done, things she had been told, each moment found its place among the flower beds and groves and lawns, until finally the *whole* garden stretched out before her. It was suddenly very clear.

And for the first time in a long time, Adele Winterbottom knew exactly what to do.

Vengeance

16

Silas emerged from his bedroom at exactly seven thirty, trailed by a very ill-tempered Thorn (who was still recovering from the effects of the chicken poisoning). Waiting patiently in the hall outside was Mrs. Hammer—there to greet the master formally and hand him Thorn's silver leash—just as she did every morning.

"I had the cook prepare some broth for you, sir," Mrs. Hammer informed him as they headed down the wide corridor toward the elevator.

"I am not hungry," said Silas, his voice weak.

"Sir, perhaps one of the servants should take Thorn for his walk. You do not look at all well."

"Nonsense," said Silas firmly. "I can do it myself."

Mrs. Hammer pushed the gold button on the elevator panel and the gilded doors slid open—the cabin glowed in a halo of morning light. As Silas entered the cage the cables released a familiar tight screech, flexing against the pulleys.

Silas stopped. Listening.

With a click of the joystick he backed out of the cage.

"Is there something wrong, sir?" asked Mrs. Hammer.

"Indeed," said Silas softly.

He picked up Thorn's heavy leash and threw it into the elevator. The metal chain and thick silver collar hit the shiny floor with a loud clunk.

Silas looked up again, staring intently into the elevator shaft.

Moments later the rope snapped in the pulley. The last threads of steel holding the rope together tore apart and the cable uncurled, flailing around the shaft and lashing the supporting columns in a volley of cracking sparks that shot out like bullets.

A thunderous groan ripped from the elevator as it began to plummet, sending a powerful gust of wind down the chamber.

Mrs. Hammer cried out.

One floor below Milo and Adele were on the landing as a furious wall of wind rushed from the shaft, nearly blowing them over. Down in the entrance hall, the staff (assembled for their morning inspection) looked up as the giant iron cage fell.

The elevator dropped...third floor...second floor...first floor...

The cage crashed to the ground with a thunderous roar, the ornate iron bars buckling like paper clips. The ground shook. A cloud of smoke blew out from the wreckage and a deep crack broke across the stone floor.

Screams erupted like sirens as the line of maids and servants broke apart. It looked like a bomb had just exploded.

On the fourth floor Silas Winterbottom was peering down into the smoky cavern of the elevator shaft, his black eyes fixed on the smoldering wreckage below.

"Mercy!" shrieked Mrs. Hammer. She coughed violently as thick clouds of smoke filled her lungs. "What on *earth* could have happened?"

"I would have thought it was obvious," said Silas calmly. "Somebody just tried to kill me."

In the oval dining room Rosemary, Milo, Adele, and Isabella sat at the far end of the grand table. Gathered behind them was every member of the household staff who had been present when the elevator crashed. They had been summoned by Detective Dickens, who was in charge of the investigation.

"This morning," began Silas from the head of the table, "an attempt was made on my life. Detective Dickens has just informed me that the elevator rope was cut with some sort of knife or sharp object. Someone was determined to give me a most violent death."

A wave of disbelief rippled across the room.

"Are you sure about this, Detective?" said Rosemary anxiously.

"Oh, yes, ma'am," confirmed the heavily bearded detective. "Mr. Winterbottom would have been crushed on impact." He made a rather vile spluttering noise with his lips. "Every bone in his body *crushed*. Like a bug."

"I don't mean that," snapped Rosemary. "I mean, are you *sure* that it was intentional?"

"No doubt at all, ma'am," said the detective somberly. "Now,

I'm going to need a statement from everyone who was here last night...including the children."

"Oh, this is too awful," sobbed Adele, covering her face.

"Surely you don't suspect us?" said Isabella, looking at the detective like he was a complete nincompoop.

"Well, to be honest with you, young lady," said Detective Dickens, "most crimes of this nature *are* committed by a family member."

"Well, in that case, look no further than Milo Winterbottom," announced Isabella, thrusting her finger across the table in the direction of her cousin. "He came to Sommerset seeking revenge against Uncle Silas—he told me so himself!"

Gasps erupted around the room.

"Isabella, that's a wicked thing to say!" said Rosemary.

"It's the truth," said Isabella confidently. "Milo came here to get even with Uncle Silas because his parents exploded. The boy is a lunatic. Ask Adele if you don't believe me."

All eyes fell upon Adele. She felt the burden of all those people staring at her...waiting on her answer. It was suffocating.

"I don't remember," she told them.

"Of course you do," snapped Isabella. "Tell them, cousin; tell them what Milo said."

"Miss Adele," said the detective sternly, "I would ask you to think very carefully about what you recall. Attempted murder is a serious business."

"Milo's not a murderer!" cried Adele. "He didn't really mean what he said. It was just…he was upset, that's all. We all say things we don't mean when we're upset, don't we?"

Detective Dickens was scribbling something down in his notebook. He stopped and looked directly at Adele. "What was it *precisely* that your cousin said?"

The room was utterly silent, every ear cocked, just waiting to devour her answer. Adele did not dare look up just in case her eyes fell upon Milo. In her rush to defend him she had said too much. Now there was no choice but to tell the truth. She felt sick.

"It's okay, Adele," said Milo suddenly, his voice small. "This is my problem and I'll deal with it." He turned to the detective. "I told my cousins that I came to Sommerset for revenge."

The room erupted in a frenzy of gasps and whispers.

"Quiet, please!" shouted the blinking detective. "There must be silence…please!"

With his eyes blanketed by a fringe of thick black hair, no one could tell where Milo was looking. His lips were tense and pale.

"Milo," said the detective carefully, "did you cut the cable on the elevator?"

"No," he said in a firm voice. "I wanted to hurt Uncle Silas for what he did to my parents, but that doesn't mean I wanted to kill him." He lifted his eyes, pushing the hair from his face and staring straight at his uncle. "My parents raised me better than that."

Silas watched him with utter fascination.

"What were your movements last night, Milo?" said Detective Dickens.

"I...I went to bed straight after dinner," he said, his voice shaking slightly. "I read a book for a while and then went to sleep."

Silas leaned forward, resting his elbows on the table. "You didn't leave your room all night, Milo?"

"Not once," he answered.

"See, Detective," declared Silas, "the boy has a perfectly reasonable alibi. You must look elsewhere for my assassin."

"Are you *kidding* me?" snarled Isabella, thumping her hand on the table. "Milo is a two-faced little orphan—you cannot believe a word he says! I demand you arrest him now before he kills us all!"

"Shut up!" shouted Milo, leaping to his feet. "I hate you! I hate all of you!"

With that, the young boy ran from the room, taking with him the heavy cloud of suspicion. He wanted to run far away but did not know where he would go. With tears stinging his face Milo hurried out of the mansion. He had never felt so alone in his entire life.

Amid the chaos that followed, the meeting came to a rapid conclusion. Most of the servants returned to their quarters to gossip about the morning's shocking events, while Rosemary went in search of Milo. Isabella disappeared shortly after, retiring to her room with Hannah Spoon to get her toenails painted.

When Milo entered the greenhouse he found himself in a lush garden teeming with lime trees, sweet peppers, and exotic ferns with leaves that spread out like butterfly wings. Down the far end of a very long aisle he found who he was looking for, hunched over, digging in a bed of turnips.

"I guess you've heard what happened," said Milo.

Moses nodded. "Police were down here asking questions." He looked at the boy. "You been crying?"

"No," said Milo defensively. He wiped at his eyes. "The detective, he doesn't think it was an accident. The thing is, last night I couldn't sleep, so I decided to take a walk in the gardens. I saw the light on in your cottage, so I came down." He paused. "I knocked, but you didn't answer."

Moses shrugged gruffly. "Didn't hear you, that's all."

"I went around back of the cottage," continued Milo, "and looked in through the window...you weren't inside, Moses."

With his index finger Moses gouged a row of holes into the soil and pushed a turnip seed into each one. "I went out—didn't get back until morning."

"Where were you?"

"None of your business," grunted the old man.

After a lengthy silence Milo said, "I know that you and Uncle Silas hate each other."

"Who told you that?" he snapped.

"I'd...I'd rather not say." Milo swallowed. "I've seen the way you two look at each other; it's pretty clear that you're not friends. So when I heard that someone had cut the elevator rope—"

"You think it was me, do ya?"

"I don't know," said Milo honestly. "Is it true—do you and Silas hate each other?"

"We're not friends," he said, scratching at his chin, "that much is true."

"Because of the car accident?"

The old man glared at him, his nostrils flaring. He dropped the bag of bulbs and stalked off.

"I know that Lady Bloom was killed and your son badly hurt," Milo called after him. "I'm sorry, Moses. I know what it feels like when something terrible happens to someone you love."

Moses stopped at the back door of the greenhouse. "I can't talk about that, Milo," he muttered.

"What are you afraid of? Has Uncle Silas threatened you?"

"Just leave it, boy," he said softly.

But Milo would not leave it. He sat down on a wooden crate and looked down at the dirt floor. "I just want to know the truth, Moses. About my uncle…about everything. I think that's why I came to Sommerset. To find the truth about my family."

"I understand, lad. Someday," said Moses, pushing his straw hat farther down on his head. "Someday, when the time is right, I'll tell you what I know. But not today."

Then Moses turned and walked back inside to plant another row of turnips.

A full moon hung high in the sky above the entrance hall, washing the cracked stone floor in soft light. Adele hurried past the wreckage that was once the elevator shaft and disappeared down a wide corridor, her bare feet pattering lightly across the floor. She crossed the final corridor and entered the anteroom.

He was waiting for her.

She gasped. Silas sat in the darkened vault, his eyes flickering in the darkness. Thorn stood guard beside his master.

"It is time for your first report, child," said Silas softly.

Her heart thumped madly in her chest. "I, um, I haven't really got a great deal to tell you, uncle. My cousins haven't done anything unusual or interesting…truly. Milo is so quiet, and Isabella, well, she spends most of her time playing with Thorn or having her hair combed."

"Adele, if you will not be honest with me, how on earth can you expect me to entrust this estate to you?"

"Honestly, Uncle Silas," Adele whispered. "I don't know anything."

"I find that rather difficult to believe." Silas stroked his chin. "Actually, I find it *impossible* to believe. You see, I recently learned that even before you agreed to spy for me, you were seen eavesdropping on Milo and that idiot Knox in the orchard. My source tells me that you were hidden from view in the arbor, while my nephew and the boy were deep in conversation." He smiled coolly. "Adele, let us not forget the dark future that awaits you at Ratchet's House if you fail. Come now, tell me what you know."

"It's nothing really," explained Adele softly. She felt utterly powerless against her uncle. He was always ten steps ahead, laying traps and playing games. It was true, she had stumbled upon Milo and Knox talking in the orchard, but she had not set out to eavesdrop. Yet, that is exactly what she did…and Silas knew it.

"Milo was asking about Moses," she confessed. "About how long he had been at Sommerset—that sort of thing."

"What else?" said Silas firmly.

"Well…he was asking about the car accident that killed Lady Bloom."

Silas leaned forward in his chair, his eyes hungry. "Go on."

"Milo seemed very curious." She shook her head. "That's all I know."

"Has Moses spoken to the boy?" he hissed. "Tell me!"

"I don't know," said Adele. "I haven't seen them together, honestly, Uncle Silas. What I told you is the truth, and that's all I know."

His face shone a ghostly white, and when Adele lifted her head to look at him something terrible and black danced behind his eyes.

"It is as I expected," he whispered. Then he closed his eyes and when he opened them again Adele saw a new softness there. "You have done well, child—but next time, do not lie to me, or I will not be so forgiving."

When Adele entered the darkened library she was still shaking. Silas's black eyes and the chill in his voice were burned into her memory. He was playing with her, she knew that now. Milo was the one he was really interested in. Not her.

Had she truly thought she had a chance of becoming the next heir of Sommerset?

Pacing in front of the black marble fireplace, Adele tried to calm herself. To think clearly. For every puzzle there was a solution—her father had always said that. Her mind flooded with visions of the cloaked Dr. Mangrove. Of the elusive basement.

If she could only find a way in. Then, perhaps, she would know how better to deal with Uncle Silas.

Looking up into the darkness of the library's towering wall of books, Adele noticed for the first time how the moonlight broke through the large windows on the upper level, sifting into a narrow shaft of light that hit a remote corner of the second-floor shelves. It looked very peculiar—this single shard of light spotlighting a small row of books...as if...as if it were pointing the way.

Then it hit her. Theodore Epstein Bloom's engraving at the threshold to the library's secret entrance.

ONLY IN DARKNESS WILL YOU SEE THE LIGHT.

Did it refer to this—a single point of moonlight cutting through the darkened library? That had to be it! Running two steps at a time, Adele raced up the narrow staircase to the second floor, sprinting around to the farthest corner of the room. The moonlight narrowed into a small round beam illuminating a narrow range of books on the bottom shelf. She crouched down and read the spines, which were glowing a silvery white. *The Complete History of String Vol. 1–6.*

Her heart sunk. *String?* What did that have to do with the secrets of Sommerset House? With little enthusiasm she grabbed volume two from the shelf. As it slid out a grinding sound, like metal wheels beginning to turn, broke the silence. Then the entire row of books split in the middle, cranking slowly back on either side like a parting curtain.

Adele could hardly believe it.

Tilting her head, she squinted into the deep recess that had opened behind it. The cavity was lined in red velvet and held a small number of tattered old books. She reached in and carefully pulled them out. They looked ancient. One by one she sorted through the titles, her hands tingling with excitement and fear—*The Journal of Theodore Epstein Bloom; How to Mind Control the One You Love; The Lost Art of Black Magic; The Science of the Soul.*

The final tome was pale blue with faded silver leaf lettering. *Sommerset House—Architectural Notes and Blueprints.* Yes! If any book could help her find a way into the basement, this was it.

Making herself more comfortable on the floor, Adele was moving the other books to one side when a name caught her eye. The book was *The Science of the Soul.* The author—Dr. Mikal Mangrove! Could it be the same Dr. Mangrove who was hiding in the basement of Sommerset? Surely it was no coincidence. Carefully, she opened the book and immediately her eyes fell upon the publication date. She froze. No.

No, it was not possible!

She read it again.

Printed in 1867. Dr. Mangrove was more than 150 years old! Trembling, Adele opened the book and began to read.

The Tables Turn

Two days passed, and the police investigation made little progress. The weapon used to cut the elevator cable had not been located, and without an eyewitness, hopes of identifying Silas's would-be assassin began to fade.

Just as life slowly returned to normal on the island, Silas's health began to deteriorate. He fainted several times in the gardens and was often breathless and unable to leave his bed.

It was clear to all that Silas was in the final stages of his illness.

Refusing to give in to the gloom of her brother's condition, Rosemary organized a special lunch in his honor to be held in the wildflower meadow. Mrs. Hammer oversaw the preparations and the kitchen created a feast of lobsters, cheese platters, leafy salads, and trays of delicious fruits from the orchard.

On the day of the picnic, the sun sat high in the pale blue sky. Isabella had insisted on escorting Silas and Thorn to the luncheon all by herself—desperate to spend as much time alone with her uncle as possible. While she no longer regarded Milo as real competition for Silas's fortune (he hated the man, after all), the same could not be said for Adele. Despite a string of disasters, Silas still seemed to take a particular interest in the little tomato head—twice Isabella had seen them whispering together in the library.

It was infuriating!

Fortunately, Isabella had a new plan. She had recently learned that her uncle was fiercely protective of a particular flower in his garden—the Phoenix rose—and would explode with rage if anyone even went near one of them. With this information in mind, Isabella convinced *dear* Adele to cut a large bunch of the Phoenix roses to decorate the table at Silas's special lunch.

Adele, still desperate to get back in her uncle's good graces after poisoning his crocodile, immediately took the bait. Wickedly, Isabella suggested that Adele write a special card to go with the flowers.

"That way," she explained, "Uncle Silas will know that the gesture was all yours!"

"Yes," said Adele eagerly, "a note. What a great idea!"

Walking through the central garden room with Silas and Thorn on their way to the lunch, Isabella stopped to admire a yellow rose.

"Oh, how beautiful!" She sighed dreamily. "It is just fortunate that Sommerset will never be mine. You see, unlike Adele, I could never change anything about the island. Not a single thing."

"Come now—surely you would change *something* about the place?"

"Never! It is paradise," she remarked, "and should remain exactly as it is today."

Silas closed his eyes and Isabella noticed how fragile he seemed.

"What a pity, child," he whispered, "that you made me promise not to consider you as my heir."

In mere seconds Isabella was kneeling by her uncle's chair, her hand gently stroking his bony arm. "But, Uncle, you know I have no need for it," she said earnestly. "Not like Adele and Milo, who are so very poor." She pointed to a group of potted fig trees beneath a stone window. "I would have more use for one of those trees than I would for Sommerset."

"Indeed," said Silas.

Isabella sighed again. "But I suppose," she said solemnly, "if you *did* have your heart set on leaving Sommerset to me...well, I would have to put my own feelings aside and accept your wishes, Uncle." She kissed his cold hand. "You know what is best, after all."

Down the meadow, under the shade of the enormous evergreen oak, a long table was laid with polished silverware and bone china. In the center stood a large crystal vase filled to the brim with flaming Phoenix roses.

When Isabella arrived with Silas and Thorn she made certain that her uncle did not go directly to the table, insisting that he sit out in the sun and rest while the final preparations were made. The idea seemed to please him, and Isabella walked with Silas down to the lake. She placed a blanket over his legs and kissed his cheek.

"I will call you when lunch is ready, Uncle," she said sweetly.

"Actually," said Silas, "I wish to have a word with you...with *all* of you. Please gather your cousins and bring them down to me."

"Now?" asked Isabella.

"Indeed."

Dutifully, Isabella returned to the oak tree. She found Adele first and congratulated her on the flowers.

"They look *wonderful*, cousin!"

"Thank you," said Adele shyly. "I had to climb the wall to get into Uncle Silas's hidden garden. I was certain Moses would catch me! Do you really think he will like them?"

"He will love them!" declared Isabella. "You wrote a card as I suggested?"

"Yes," said Adele. "I just hope he is pleased this time."

"I am sure of it, cousin," said Isabella reassuringly. She looked about the meadow. "Now where on earth is the orphan? Uncle Silas wants to speak with all of us before lunch."

Once Milo was located (he was found wandering around near the greenhouse), the three cousins headed down to the lake to meet with their uncle.

"There is something you should know," announced Silas without delay. "From tonight on, your bedrooms will have to be locked from the outside. This measure is being taken for your own safety."

"You can't do that!" said Milo angrily. "We are not prisoners!"

"It does seem rather extreme, Uncle," said Isabella more gently.

"It is for your own protection," said Silas matter-of-factly. "There is an assassin somewhere on the island, and until that person is captured, I must do everything I can to protect you." Turning his back and moving away from the children, he added, "In time you will get used to it."

Adele had a terrible feeling. After her discovery in the library, she knew that Uncle Silas was planning something truly awful, and she did not believe for one minute that locking them up at night had anything to do with the attempt on his life. She wanted to say something to her cousins, to warn them, but before she could, Rosemary called everyone to come and sit down.

As the maids began serving lunch, Silas took his position at the head of the table. It took only seconds for him to notice the crystal vase brimming with murdered Phoenix roses. His face froze in an expression of disbelief and rage.

Adele and Isabella exchanged excited glances as Silas reached for the small white envelope at the base of the vase and tore it open.

"Do read it aloud, Uncle!" urged Isabella. She could hardly contain her excitement—surely Silas would have Adele flogged and thrown from the island for this!

"Very well," hissed Silas. "The card says, *From your loving niece…Isabella.*"

Instantly the satisfied smile fell from Isabella's face, replaced with a look of extreme confusion.

"What?" she shrieked. "Um, Uncle…don't you mean, *From your loving niece Adele?*"

"No, I do not." Silas threw the card at her. He looked pained as he continued to stare at his beloved flowers, blooming in shades of orange and red like a hundred heads of fire.

"These flowers are precious," he seethed, his teeth glistening like fangs. "How *dare* you touch them, Isabella! You stupid little imbecile!"

Isabella began to tremble.

"But...Uncle...there has been a mistake. You see..." But she could not explain. Not without revealing her role in the whole dreadful business. She was trapped.

Adele leaned over to her cousin and whispered, "You have helped me so much, Isabella. It didn't seem right that I keep taking all the credit for your wonderful ideas." She smiled sweetly. "This is just my way of saying thank you, *cousin*."

Isabella gasped.

"Why, you little freckled-face freak!" she spat, her nostrils flaring. "I'll get you for this, I swear I will!" She turned to face her uncle like a guilty prisoner awaiting her sentence. "Uncle, you must understand that I did not do—"

"Do not say another word!" Silas snapped, interrupting her. "I think it would be best if you returned to your room at once."

"But, Uncle—"

"Go!" hissed Silas, his black eyes swelling with rage. Isabella jumped up, knocking her chair to the ground and running toward the house, crying loudly the whole way.

"They're only flowers, for goodness sake," said Rosemary with a scowl.

"No, they are not!" declared Silas. "They are *everything!*" He backed away from the table. "I have lost my appetite," he said curtly. "You must continue without me."

With the guest of honor gone, Rosemary called her brother several awful names before grabbing two large lobsters and a cheese platter and stomping off toward the summerhouse. Next to go was Milo. He had still not forgiven Adele for conspiring with Isabella to make him a suspect in the elevator crash. He left without a word.

Adele looked somberly around the abandoned table.

When Isabella first came to her and suggested she pick the Phoenix roses for Uncle Silas, Adele was already awake to her cousin's true motive. That horrible night after Thorn was poisoned, Adele had looked back over everything that had happened since she arrived on the island and her cousin's manipulation was suddenly, shockingly clear...Isabella had been playing her for a fool since day one! Every kind word, every piece of helpful advice—it had all been one gigantic trick!

And if Adele had any doubts about her theory they vanished when Isabella encouraged her to pick the flowers her uncle loved so much. Cutting Silas's beloved Phoenix roses, killing them, was hardly going please him. It didn't make sense. Actually, it *did* make sense. Isabella wasn't trying to help Adele; she was trying to destroy her chances. Not only was her cousin a thief and a liar, she was scheming to get Sommerset all for herself!

Hurt and anger fueled her decision to get even with Isabella for all the horrible things she had done—and it had worked. Isabella had been disgraced in Uncle Silas's eyes. And yet, getting even hadn't taken away the deep unease coiled in the pit of her stomach. In fact, it had only intensified since her shocking discovery in the library. It was the same unease she had tried to bury that first morning when a passing cloud had revealed Sommerset House as a great squatting beast, its sharp talons poised to strike.

Only now was she beginning to understand what that gruesome vision had been trying to tell her—the monster poised to strike was Silas Winterbottom.

Midnight Caller

Two candles mounted in a silver bracket on the wall illuminated the library in a soft apricot glow. Silas sat under the flickering light with his eyes closed, his right hand stroking the rough scales of Thorn's head.

He was waiting.

"Sorry I am late, Uncle," she said, rushing into the room.

Silas's eyes flicked open, two dark globes glistening in the dim light.

"As am I," said Silas sharply. "After what you did today, consider it a small miracle that you are even here, child."

"Yes, Uncle. I'm very sorry—"

"Silence. I am in no mood for groveling. It is late, and you should be locked up safely in your bedroom like your cousins. I trust you have a *very* good reason for requesting this meeting."

"Yes, Uncle. You see, I must tell you that there is a thief in the house."

"A thief?" said Silas slowly.

She nodded. "They have stolen silverware, clocks...all kinds of things. I've seen her stealing with my own eyes." She stopped, her voice breaking up. “I don’t want to get anybody in trouble, but I can’t keep it from you any longer.”

Silas observed his niece with great interest, his pallid face suddenly more vibrant than it had been in days. “I am very pleased that you have come to me with this.” He rubbed at his lips. “Now tell me, child, who is the thief?”

“It is Adele,” she said, the glow from the flickering candle dancing across her face. “I saw her take the silverware at dinner last week.” Isabella wiped at her eyes. “Oh, Uncle, I never thought someone as kind and gentle as Adele could steal from her own family!”

“Indeed,” remarked Silas. “I must confess that after you mutilated my roses, I had no desire to see your face ever again.” He took a shallow breath. “But you have impressed me, Isabella; turning in your cousin like this takes considerable…courage.”

“What will happen now?” Isabella asked. “What will you do to her?”

“I will do what needs to be done.”

Rosemary dug into the deep pockets of her dressing gown, finding two walnuts and a hairpin. She replaced the hairpin and began to munch enthusiastically on the nuts, humming all the while. From the glass dome high above her, moonlight bathed the entrance hall in a pearly glow. Even Rosemary’s mass of tangled red hair looked soft and pale. She stepped over one of the deeper cracks in the floor, twirling around playfully as she went.

"Does the state of my floor amuse you, Rosemary?"

The chunky woman was startled, letting out a gasp. "Good lord! You nearly scared the life out of me, Silas!"

"Indeed." He moved his chair over the web of fractures spun across the stone floor. "I thought you retired to bed?"

"Couldn't sleep," she said simply, picking a piece of walnut from her massive front teeth. "Who can *sleep* with all the nonsense going on in this house? Crashing elevators, assassins on the loose, young children *locked* in their bedrooms. Honestly, Silas, is that really necessary?"

"It is," said Silas firmly. "As you delight in pointing out—there is a killer on the loose. I have a moral duty to protect Isabella, Milo, and Adele, and that is what I am doing."

"Which is all very noble, Silas," said Rosemary with a roll of her big dark eyes. "But as I recall, the assassin tried to kill you, not them. Seems to me, you've locked the wrong person in their bedroom chamber."

Silas covered his mouth and yawned. "How witty you are, sister."

"Something has been troubling me," said Rosemary, regarding her brother carefully. "And forgive me for saying this, Silas, but why on earth would someone go to all the effort of killing a man who is already dying? As a student of human nature, I would think that such a person must be filled with rage. Who on earth could hate you *that* much?"

Silas closed his eyes and took a shallow breath. "The assassin is insane," he said slowly. "Who knows what twisted reason they may have conjured? I am a wealthy man, sister, and hate is drawn to wealth as bees are to honey. Anyone…anyone at all might have marked me for death." He opened his eyes and glared darkly at her. "Even you."

"Me?" Rosemary let out a snort. "Why on earth would I want to kill you?"

"Neglect, envy, spite," said Silas coolly. "Take your pick. I ignored you for thirty years, and suddenly you turn up uninvited, demanding to stay. Then just days later an attempt is made on my life. The timing is rather interesting, don't you think?"

Rosemary smiled, her teeth flaring under the moonlight. "Silas, if I really was the assassin, you would already be dead."

"Would I?" His black eyes were locked into hers.

"Oh, *yes*, pet," whispered Rosemary. She took three short steps toward her brother's chair, looking over him. "I spent two years in the Amazon—met the most *wonderful* tribe living along the Japurá River. What they don't know about poisonous plants wasn't worth knowing. A few drops in your milk and your heart would stop within thirty seconds. And the best part of all? The poison leaves no trace."

"You seem to have given my death a great deal of thought."

"Not really," said Rosemary with a shrug. "I'm just pointing out that if I was going to kill you, I certainly wouldn't need to crush a perfectly good elevator in the process. You look tired, brother." She kissed Silas on the forehead. "We can talk again in the morning. Here's an idea—I'll cook you an old-fashioned breakfast, just like Mother used to make us when we were children. Do you remember?"

"I do," said Silas softly.

Rosemary licked her lips. "Fried bacon and mushrooms, poached eggs, and a lovely tall glass of *milk.*"

Throwing her brother a wicked grin, Rosemary departed. Silas watched thoughtfully as his sister ambled across the vast entrance hall and disappeared down a lengthy corridor, the loud thump of her heavy steps fading into a deathly silence.

Adele was perched on a broad tree limb peering through the curtains of Milo's bedroom window. She had been out there for several minutes, gathering courage. Carefully she stepped onto the window ledge. With her right hand she parted the curtain and looked into the room.

Milo's bed was empty. She leaned in for a closer look. Milo *had* to be there—his door was locked just like hers. Where could he have gone? Suddenly a hand gripped her wrist, pulling her through the window. She fell to the floor with a thump.

"Why are you spying on me?" Milo demanded to know.

Adele pulled her arm from Milo's grip.

"I wasn't spying!" said Adele as she got to her feet. "I need your help."

Milo gazed at her suspiciously. It's not that he disliked his cousin—she'd been rather nice to him, in fact—but he didn't trust her. He didn't trust anyone. "Help with what?"

"Stopping Uncle Silas," she said simply.

He hadn't expected that. Milo only had to look into his cousin's eyes to see that she wasn't kidding around. All of a sudden he was *very* interested in what Adele had to say. "Okay, I'm listening."

The girl sat down on the bed and took a deep breath before beginning.

"The first thing you should know is that Uncle Silas asked me to spy on you and Isabella...and I agreed." Before Milo could react, Adele pressed on, letting the whole story tumble out—about Ratchet's House and Uncle Silas's threats and the carving in the floor and the hidden shelf and what she had read in Dr. Mangrove's book.

"Uncle Silas brought Mangrove here for a reason," she explained. "He's old, Milo—really, *really* old—and he has all these crazy ideas about the human soul. See, he's invented some sort of chamber; only that chapter was torn out of the book and I don't know what it does. What I do know is that Uncle Silas is planning something really bad...and somehow we're a part of it."

Milo looked at her doubtfully.

"Crazy scientists, hidden shelves, missing chapters—why should I believe any of this?" he said bluntly. "For all I know this is just some insane story you and Isabella whipped up to trick me."

"Isabella has been working against me since I got here," declared Adele. "What I'm telling you is true. Look around, Milo, Uncle Silas has locked us up, the phones aren't working. He has sealed us off from the world. Do you really think he invited us here out of the goodness of his heart? We're trapped on this island, Milo. We're trapped whether you want to believe it or not."

"I can leave anytime I want to," declared Milo.

"No, you can't," said Adele sadly. "The truth is...I don't think Uncle Silas intends for any of us to leave. Not ever."

Milo saw the certainty and terror on his cousin's face, and it scared him to death.

"You know how I feel about Uncle Silas," he said, sitting down next to her on the bed, "and the truth is, I have my own suspicions about him. You've heard about the car accident that killed his fiancée, Lady Bloom?"

Adele nodded. "She left him Sommerset in her will."

"Well, I'm not so sure it *was* an accident. I don't have proof yet, but I'm working on it."

"We need to stop him, Milo," said Adele more urgently. "Dr. Mangrove is building something in the basement—I heard Mrs. Hammer and Bingle talking about it. Only I haven't found a way down yet. I know where the blueprints for the house are hidden, but I'm going to need your help making sense of them." She held out her hand. "Come with me, and I'll show you."

Milo hesitated, but only for a second. He quickly realized there was really no choice but to work with Adele. Uncle Silas was planning something horrendous, and he had to be stopped—it seemed their very lives were at stake.

After a brief nod of his head, Milo got up and climbed onto the ledge with his cousin.

Trying hard not to look down, Adele jumped first, grabbing the thick bough directly above her head. She moved easily between branches and reached the outer limbs of the tree's summit in moments.

Following his cousin's lead, Milo jumped out toward the sycamore. He landed clumsily, thumping his hip against a thick knot on the tree branch. He steadied himself, down on hands and knees like a cat. Carefully he arched his neck, as if he were howling at the moon, spotting Adele in the upper branches.

"Come on," Adele whispered, "it's easy once you start!"

"If you say so," he replied doubtfully.

Shakily, Milo crawled along the large twisted bough. He grabbed a nearby limb and managed to get onto his feet, splaying his legs along the branch to steady himself. With trembling hands, he grasped the limb above and slowly pulled himself up. Before he was even aware it was happening, Milo was climbing swiftly through the tree.

When he finally reached Adele his arms were aching.

"Did I mention I'm scared of heights?" he whispered, his breathing rapid.

Adele smiled. "You did great."

"If it's okay with you," said Milo with a grin, "I'd really like to get out of this tree."

"We just need to climb up to that next branch," she said, pointing the way. "We can reach the window on the second-floor landing from there."

Milo stood up and took his hand from the overhanging branch as he adjusted his footing. "Lead the way," he whispered. "The sooner I'm on solid ground—"

Silence.

Adele looked over. He was gone. His muffled screams exploded from underneath her and Adele looked down just in time to see her cousin smash against a thick branch and tumble down, his body jolting as he hit the ground.

"Milo!"

Adele swung from limb to limb until she was low enough to leap to the ground. She knelt over Milo's body, his arms and legs twisted and tangled like a rag doll. A river of blood flowed from underneath his body.

She screamed and lights began to illuminate like spot fires all over Sommerset House.

Aftermath

"He is dead," said Isabella, tears pooling beneath her blue eyes.

"No, please don't say that," cried Adele. "Milo can't be dead."

She slumped down onto the floor outside Milo's bedroom and leaned her head against the wall.

"What on earth were you two doing up a tree?" Isabella asked her cousin yet again. "It does seem very strange, cousin."

"I told you...we were just talking," was all Adele could manage in response.

"Talking in a tree at *midnight?*" said Isabella doubtfully. Then she smiled softly. "Poor Adele! You must feel so dreadfully guilty. After all, Milo wouldn't be lying in there close to death if you hadn't made him climb that silly tree." She patted her on the head. "Still, you mustn't blame yourself."

Adele covered her face and began to cry. It *was* all her fault, and she knew it.

When the medical team arrived from the hospital they immediately braced Milo's neck and had him moved upstairs to his bedroom chamber for a thorough examination. It was early afternoon before his door opened again.

Both girls looked up at the same time as Rosemary stepped out into the corridor.

"How is he?" cried Adele, jumping to her feet.

"Milo's dead, isn't he, Aunt Rosemary?" Isabella wailed. "That poor little orphan has crossed over to the spirit world!"

"He hasn't crossed anywhere," said Rosemary firmly. "Your cousin is alive and well, but he has been badly injured. He has a broken leg and a lot of bruising on his back and arms. You can go in and see him—but only one at a time. Doctor's orders."

"He's going to be all right?" asked Adele anxiously.

"He will be." She wiped the tears from Adele's face. "He's asked to see you."

"He has?" Her eyes widened. "Is he angry with me?"

Rosemary smiled. "Go and find out for yourself."

As Adele approached the bed she studied Milo carefully—his black hair falling lazily around his face, his plastered leg propped up under a pillow. There were cuts on his chin and a bruise on his left cheek. One of his fingers was bandaged, and she saw a dark purple bruise covering his right arm like a tattoo.

"Are you…does it hurt much?" she asked.

"No," said Milo, "not too much. Just a little."

"Milo, I'm so sorry," she said, the tears once again falling down her face. "You are hurt because of me. You could have died! This is all my fault!"

"No, it's not, Adele," declared Milo firmly. "It was my choice to jump out that window; no one made me do it." He glanced over at the group of nurses and doctors who were busy packing away their equipment and lowered his voice. "Besides, we had a good reason for being out there last night. Nothing's changed, Adele—we still have to stop Uncle Silas."

"I was hoping you would say that," said Adele, relieved. "In fact, I have an idea that just might work. Listen—"

Just then the door opened and Bingle entered the room. Stiffly, he crossed the floor and stood against the far wall with his arms folded behind his back.

"Um, Bingle," said Milo, after a few moments, "what are you doing?"

"Your uncle has asked that I keep an eye on you." He smiled, but it was hardly convincing. "Just to make sure you don't suffer a relapse. Don't worry, sir; you won't even know I'm here."

"I don't need a baby-sitter," said Milo firmly.

"Of course not, sir," explained Bingle. "This is purely a precaution. As you know, there is an assassin running about the place, and I suppose your uncle is worried."

Realizing that they would no longer be able to speak privately, Adele announced that she had better leave so that Isabella could come in and visit.

"Thanks for coming," said Milo. "And remember, none of this is your fault."

"I'll try. Thanks, Milo." Adele leaned down and kissed her cousin on the cheek.

"I'll come back after dark," she whispered in his ear. "Leave the window open. We don't have much time left."

"You have seen the boy?"

"I have. Bingle alerted me as soon as the medical team returned to the hospital," said Dr. Mangrove, placing his medical bag on a table beside Silas's bed. "Milo was given a sleeping pill with his dinner, so there was no danger."

"Will he recover fully?" said Silas tensely.

"He will," confirmed the doctor. "Apart from his injuries, the boy is in perfect health."

A look of relief swept across Silas's ashen face. "We can proceed then."

"Most definitely."

"Now tell me about the elixir," said Silas, his eyes glistening wildly. "Were you able to salvage any of the roses my idiotic niece cut up?"

"Most of them," said Dr. Mangrove. "However, it was a complicated matter. The cell structure of the Phoenix rose is very temperamental. Extracting the elixir was never going to be easy." His small eyes clouded over. "If *only* I had more of the panacea; from that miraculous plant all things are possible. As it is, I have barely enough to survive the year."

"We will get more, Mangrove," said Silas with certainty. "You have my word. But the elixir…there is enough for our purposes?"

"Yes...but only just." Dr. Mangrove pulled the small glass bottle from his jacket and held it up to the light. "This is all we have... every drop."

"Give it to me," said Silas, eyeing the elixir greedily. He held out his trembling hand, and Dr. Mangrove gently placed it on his palm.

"Every single drop is precious," the doctor reminded him. "It has taken several lifetimes to finally produce a perfect batch."

Silas eased his frail body up and placed his bony finger under the side table next to his bed. A wooden panel slid back from the headboard. Carefully Silas placed the elixir into the compartment before shutting it again.

"When can we begin, Doctor?"

"The chamber should be ready by tomorrow."

Silas smiled darkly. "Excellent."

The Way Down

After dinner Adele returned to the eastern wing and knocked on Milo's bedroom door. As usual Bingle answered.

"Yes, Miss Adele?"

"I've come to see Milo," she told him, trying to peek over Bingle's shoulder to catch a glimpse of her cousin.

"I'm sorry, Miss Adele, he is still sleeping."

"You said that three hours ago," said Adele, unable to hide her frustration. "Can't I just come in and sit awhile?"

"That's very thoughtful of you, Miss," said Bingle, "but I have strict instructions that Milo is not to be disturbed. Perhaps you could come back in the morning?"

"I guess so," she replied doubtfully.

All afternoon she had been troubled by a strange feeling—Milo was in danger, and she could not wait until after dark to see him. In an effort to ease her worry she had tried several times to visit her cousin, but every time Bingle had an excuse why she could not.

The Butler was trying to keep them apart, she was sure of it.

"Well, good night, Miss," said Bingle as he closed the door in her face. Then she heard the key turn in the lock.

Moments later, Adele took off down the corridor breaking into a sprint.

She was going to find a way into the basement even if it killed her.

ℓℓℓℓ

Isabella had been looking for her cousin all over Sommerset House, and when she got to the library and found a pile of moldy old books strewn across the floor beneath a concealed bookshelf, she knew that something suspicious was going on. But *what?*

She searched the library and the drawing room but found no trace of Adele. Frustrated, and rather hungry, Isabella headed for the kitchen—an apple and a cup of iced tea was just the tonic she needed to clear her head and figure out what her cousin was up to. Turning down the long hallway of the east wing, Isabella caught sight of a wild mop of tomato-colored hair disappearing around the corner. Adele!

But where on earth was the silly girl going?

Then it hit her. The basement—that *had* to be it.

Adele had found a way in!

Suddenly a great many things made sense to Isabella—including why Adele and Milo had been up in that tree last night. They must be in on it together. Yes, that had to be it! Those double-crossing little rodents had made a pact to find Uncle Silas's priceless treasures and split the loot fifty-fifty.

As Isabella stomped down the wide corridor, her blood was boiling. How dare they cut her out? She was family, after all.

Isabella stalked toward the storeroom door and threw it open. Inside the dimly lit room she was confronted by Adele's terrified eyes blinking back at her.

"Isabella, you scared me!" said Adele, her voice shaking. She was holding a large book in one hand and a lantern in the other. "I thought you were—"

"Uncle Silas?" interrupted Isabella. "I know what you are up to, cousin. You and that homicidal orphan are trying to steal Uncle Silas's hidden treasures—I'm ashamed of you both!" She looked around. "Where is your partner in crime?"

"Put a sock in it, Isabella," snapped Adele as she shut the storeroom door. "The only thief in this house is you."

Isabella gasped. "Me? How dare you! I am not a thief!"

"Of course you are," said Adele matter-of-factly. "But that's not important right now. Uncle Silas is going to hurt Milo and I'm certain it's connected to what Dr. Mangrove is building in the basement. That's why we have to find a way in."

Isabella frowned. "What do you mean, *hurt Milo?*"

"I'm not exactly sure," admitted Adele. "I just know that Dr. Mangrove has all these twisted theories, and Uncle Silas brought him here for a reason. Milo is locked in his room, and they won't let me see him. Something is very wrong, Isabella."

"Cousin, do I look stupid to you?" she said sharply. "The truth is, you are looking for Uncle Silas's pile of gold, and you're trying to cut me out. Well, it's not going to—"

"Please, Isabella, just for a moment try not to be such a brat!"

Isabella's mouth fell open, but amazingly she did not speak.

"This isn't about money or treasure or who will inherit Uncle Silas's fortune," said Adele sternly. "It's about something dark and awful happening underneath our feet. Milo needs our help, and we are going to give it to him."

"You're serious, aren't you, cousin?" said Isabella slowly. "Milo's really in trouble?"

"I think we all are," whispered Adele, "and that's why we have to find out what's going on in the basement." She handed the book to Isabella. "The blueprints clearly show that the only entrance to the basement is in this room. But so far, I can't find any sign of it."

Isabella glanced at the faded yellow pages. They showed a labyrinth of tunnels underneath the mansion and a set of stairs located in the southern corner of the storeroom. But if they had been there once, they certainly weren't there any longer.

"It doesn't make sense," said Isabella, glancing around the cluttered room stacked with crates and overstuffed boxes. "How does an entrance just disappear?"

Adele held a finger to her lips. "Shh!"

A scraping sound, like a box being pulled along the ground, was coming from a darkened corner of the room. Isabella froze. Trembling, Adele stepped forward, holding the lantern out in front of her. The storeroom fell quiet again.

Adele let out a sigh of relief. "Probably just a mouse."

"A *mouse?*" said Isabella, looking terrified.

Then he emerged from the darkness into the lantern's warm glow. He was grinning.

"Looking for something, children?"

Isabella screamed.

"Uncle Silas! No, we weren't looking for anything," she said nervously. "Adele and I were just...playing hide-and-seek. It's such fun, isn't it, cousin?"

"No," said Adele firmly. She did her best to swallow the fear rising in her throat. "We were looking for a way into the basement."

"Were you indeed?" said Silas coolly.

Adele nodded. "You see, we know what's going on down there." It was a lie, but Adele was desperate. If she could make Uncle Silas believe that they already knew what he was planning, then perhaps he might reveal what was *really* going on. "We know all about Dr. Mangrove and his building project. We know everything, Uncle Silas."

"Excellent work, Adele," he sneered, his dark eyes sparkling with pure hatred. "You have no idea how much I want to believe you, but alas, I cannot. The truth is, child, if you really knew what was going on in the basement you would not be looking for a way down." He shook his head, his eyes never leaving her. "You would be running far, far away."

Suddenly Isabella exploded into a loud laugh. "Oh, dear—Adele's lost her mind! I blame all those books she reads." Slowly stepping back, Isabella began edging toward the door. "Don't worry, Uncle; I don't believe any of it. Adele is just confused, that is all. I suggest you have her locked up in an asylum until she sees sense. That seems fair, don't you think?"

Swiftly Silas moved his chair forward, blocking the doorway. Isabella screamed, jumping back.

"Don't be in such a rush, child," said Silas coolly. "Let us *bond* for a while—that's what families do, is it not? Perhaps we could start by discussing the stolen property my security staff discovered in Adele's closet a short time ago."

Adele gasped. "What...stolen property?"

"Tell her, Isabella," said Silas softly. "Tell her what you did."

But Isabella could not speak. In fact, she could not even *look* at her cousin.

"Isabella?" said Adele, confused. "I don't understand. What's going on?"

"Valuable items have been steadily disappearing from the house," explained Silas. "Isabella discovered the identity of the thief and bravely brought that information to me. This evening while you were at dinner, Adele, all of the missing items were located in your closet." He rubbed at his pale lips. "Naturally, I will have to alert the police."

"But I didn't do it," declared Adele, looking at her cousin with a mixture of hurt and fury. "Tell him, Isabella! I never stole anything! I wouldn't!"

"Oh?" said Silas. "Then who did?"

"Well...I can't say." She closed her eyes. "I mean, I don't know."

"What a shame," said Silas. "You are sure to be Ratchet's House newest inmate now."

"Ratchet's House?" said Isabella anxiously.

"It is a place where unwanted children are locked away," explained Silas triumphantly. "That is where your cousin is to be sent when she returns to Tipping Point empty-handed. Isn't that so, Adele?"

Adele found herself nodding.

As she watched her cousin, Isabella's face grew pale. Adele was going to be locked away? No, surely not! Who would do such a thing to their own daughter?

"So, Adele," said Silas softly, "I will ask you one more time—if you are not the thief, then who is?"

Exposing Isabella as the real thief would be simple, but Adele knew that if she did that then in some strange way Silas would have won. He thrived on dividing people, turning one person against the other, breeding hatred. But today he would not have his victory. Adele would not give it to him.

"I could tell you, Uncle Silas," she replied honestly, "but I'm not going to."

Silas regarded her coldly. "Foolish child."

An uncomfortable sensation stirred and shook Isabella and she did not like it one bit. Adele was covering for her; sacrificing her freedom to protect the very person who had set her up. Isabella gasped. It reached out and up, and she could not stop it.

"Then I will send for the police immediately," she heard Silas announce.

"Wait!" cried Isabella. "I was wrong. It wasn't Adele who stole from you...it was Mrs. Hammer."

"Mrs. Hammer?" Silas looked delighted.

"Isabella," said Adele anxiously, "what are you doing?"

"That's right, Mrs. Hammer," said Isabella quickly. "The poor dear can't help herself; she steals anything that isn't nailed to the floor. I caught her red-handed lifting the silverware and she started crying like a baby, begging me not to say anything. I guess I felt sorry for her—she's so old and unattractive. I'm sorry I lied about Adele, it was a dreadful thing to do."

"This is a *surprise*," said Silas with a dark grin. "Mrs. Hammer has been such a faithful servant these last forty years. I shall send for her now and force a confession. Of course, we will have to lock her up until the police arrive."

"Is that really necessary, Uncle?" said Isabella, gulping. "I gave the old bat a very stern talking-to and she promised to *never* do it again. I think it would be far more sensible to just drop the whole thing and pretend it never happened. Don't you agree, Uncle?"

"No," said Silas coldly, his grin slipping away. "I do not. Her life as a free woman ends today. With your testimony, Isabella, I will make sure that Mrs. Hammer is locked away until her dying day."

"You can't do that." Isabella lowered her head and the soft groan that escaped from her mouth was the sound of surrender. "Mrs. Hammer didn't steal from you," she said slowly. "Neither did Adele. It was me. I'm the one."

Silas closed his eyes and laughed softly.

"Well, of course you are," he told her. "You are a thief just as your father is—I knew that before you set foot on Sommerset. You befriend wealthy girls, get yourself invited to their homes, and then steal from them. That is your modus operandi, is it not?"

As Silas spoke, Isabella felt like he had cut her open and exposed her soul to the whole world. The shame washed across her face in a river of deep crimson.

"You are a fraud, Isabella Winterbottom," declared Silas. "A common criminal; little more than a glorified pickpocket. And that is all you ever will be."

"That's not true!" shouted Adele, stepping forward to challenge her uncle. "Isabella may be a thief and a two-faced liar and a stuck-up princess, but when it really mattered, she told the truth." She turned and looked at her cousin. "If you ask me, that counts for something."

Despite the fact that her cousin had just called her a variety of unpleasant names, Isabella smiled. "Thank you, cousin."

"Family unity," said Silas with a disappointed sigh. "How very dull."

"Enough!" Adele shouted angrily at her uncle. "You're just trying to distract us, and it won't work. We know you are hiding something down in the basement, and we won't leave this room until you show us what it is!" She folded her arms and stared directly at her uncle. "I mean it, Uncle Silas. Show us what you are hiding… or else."

"Take us to the basement, you revolting old bag of bones!" declared Isabella, stamping her foot for added effect.

Silas smiled thinly.

"As you wish."

Reaching into his coat pocket, Silas grasped a small remote control and pushed on it. Immediately the stone floor beneath Adele and Isabella fell away, and before they were aware what was happening, the two girls dropped through the trapdoor, swallowed into darkness.

The Departed

Milo was up before the sun. Although his cuts and bruises still hurt, he felt a great deal better after such a long sleep. With Bingle snoring loudly in the armchair by the window, Milo dressed quietly, careful not to wake him. When he was done he tucked his crutches under his arms and headed straight for Adele's bedroom.

He wanted to know if she had made any progress regarding Dr. Mangrove.

Milo knocked on her door. No answer. He knocked again and entered.

"Adele, you awake yet?"

The room was empty. Completely empty. Adele's clothes, her books... *everything* was gone. Apart from the bed and an armchair, the bedroom was bare.

It made no sense. Milo's pulse quickened.

Hopping down the corridor, he threw open Isabella's bedroom door.

Empty.

The cold hand of fear wrapped its claws around his heart.

His cousins had vanished without a trace.

Mrs. Hammer walked quickly across the second-floor landing wearing a deep scowl. She hated sneaking about, but what choice did she have? When an old friend asks you for a favor…well, you do what you can to help. Besides, the master would not be awake yet, so she was safe enough.

Turning toward the east wing, the old housekeeper nearly jumped out of her skin when Silas appeared from behind a large marble column.

"Sir!" she gasped, clutching her chest. "Oh, dear! You startled me."

"How unfortunate," said Silas, his dark eyes staring intently at her. He pointed to a piece of paper clutched in her right hand. "What have you got there, Mrs. Hammer?"

"Oh…this? Well it's…it's a note, sir," she told him. "Just a note."

"Who is the note *for*, Mrs. Hammer?"

"Well… " She hesitated. "It's for Master Milo, sir."

Silas put out his bony hand. "Give it to me."

Dutifully Mrs. Hammer handed over the note, and Silas opened it carefully.

Milo,

Meet me by the cottage, tomorrow morning at sunrise. I reckon it's time you knew the truth about your uncle.

Moses

Silas folded the note and slipped it into his pocket. "I will see that my nephew gets it, Mrs. Hammer. You may go back to the kitchen. Oh, and, Mrs. Hammer—if you value your position here at Sommerset, keep your distance from Moses. The old man is deranged."

"Yes, sir."

"Just a moment, Mrs. Hammer," called Silas, waving her back. "Send someone down to the orchard to fetch Knox. Tell him to meet me in my study at noon. I have a job for him."

Mrs. Hammer nodded and walked swiftly to the stairs. She was in such a hurry to get away she did not notice Milo storming along the western corridor with a look of thunder in his eyes.

"Where are they, Uncle Silas?" the boy demanded, hopping toward his uncle as fast as his crutches would take him. "What have you done with my cousins?"

"Ah, yes, your cousins," said Silas calmly. "They are gone, Milo. They left last night while you were sleeping."

"Left?" Milo did not try to hide his fury. "I don't believe you!"

"You don't? Well, that is the truth, child, whether you believe it or not." Silas moved along the landing, then stopped, turning back to face his nephew. "I was hoping I wouldn't have to tell you this," he said. "But your cousins were stealing from me. Yes, that's right—stealing. I discovered their crimes and confronted them. They confessed everything."

"Adele wouldn't steal," declared Milo firmly. "You're lying, Uncle Silas. I know you are. Where are they? Now tell me where they are!"

Silas sighed wearily. "Do you know why Isabella and Adele came to Sommerset? They came for my fortune, Milo. I don't blame them, of course; their parents are vultures. However, once I was alerted to the stealing, I had no choice but to ask them to leave. I chose not to call the police." Silas smiled thinly. "Returning to their parents is punishment enough."

"It makes no sense," said Milo, shaking his head. "Adele wouldn't have left without talking to me first. She wouldn't have."

Silas laughed softly, his pallid face buckling in a wave of creases.

"What do you think I've done with them, Milo?" he said softly. "Locked them away somewhere? Come now, do you really think me capable of harming my own nieces?" He reached out for his nephew's hand, but the boy pulled away. "I'm not a monster, Milo. Just a sick old man trying to do what is right. Look, you can phone your cousins tomorrow and see that they have arrived home safely. Now that's fair, isn't it?"

Milo looked down at his hands. He wanted to cry but stopped himself. Adele and Isabella needed him, and he wasn't going to let them down.

"Yes, Uncle," he said, nodding his head, "that's fair."

Deep under Sommerset House a labyrinth of tunnels spread out like a spiderweb. Down there, the chilled air had the pungent stench of rotting fish. The walls were damp and a small stream of water trickled along the tunnel floor on a carpet of silky moss.

The prisoners were being held in a remote tunnel under the east wing.

"This is just *great*," groaned Isabella, yanking on her chains. "I thought Uncle Silas's basement was supposed to be full of gold and jewels and priceless treasures. The only priceless thing down here is *me!*"

The girls were secured to the floor by a thick chain connected to leather straps clasped around their wrists. They stood side by side midway along an enormous stretch of tunnel that narrowed to a hazy ball of dim light at the far end.

"Uncle Silas is going to pay for this!" shrieked Isabella. "My father will be furious when he finds out what that horrid man has done to me! Oh, cousin, my arms hurt, and this *smell*. If I don't get out of here, I'm going to throw up!"

Adele said nothing. She had barely spoken since waking up on the tunnel floor, chained like an animal. Her mind was a tangle of muddy thoughts, churning like a mixing bowl. Had anyone discovered they were missing yet? Was Milo okay? Was he even alive?

"How much longer are we going to be stuck down here?" whined Isabella. "He can't keep us chained up forever." She looked at her cousin, seeking a little reassurance. "He can't, can he, cousin?"

"I don't know," answered Adele. "I really don't."

Suddenly the tunnel went black. Then a flicker of light began to break the darkness like a torch being switched on and off. Both girls looked down the tunnel and saw the unmistakable silhouette of their uncle moving steadily toward them. He had a box on his lap and was tossing large pieces of raw chicken and water buffalo along the tunnel floor as he went.

"What on earth is he doing?" said Isabella nervously.

Before Adele could answer, Silas came to a stop just beyond his nieces' reach. He observed them carefully, a boyish grin spread across his ghostly face.

"Captivity suits you, Adele," he said crisply. "The fear and anger in your eyes is actually rather beautiful. It almost makes one forget about your hair. And you, Isabella, after so many years of crime, how does it feel to finally be in chains?"

"You deranged skeleton!" spat Isabella. "I may be a criminal, but at least I'm not *crazy!*"

Gazing anxiously at the trail of raw meat lining the tunnel, Adele said, "Uncle Silas, what are going to do to us?"

"Nothing, child," Silas told her softly. "I am not going to do a thing." He sighed. "However, I cannot say the same for my alligators. You see this tunnel connects directly to the swamp and in exactly one hour the gates will open and my alligators will be free to come in—it will be lunchtime, so naturally the poor beasts will be starving." Silas tipped the box upside down and a pool of animal blood splashed across the tunnel floor. "The meat is just an incentive; *you* are the main meal, and I am quite sure the reptiles will find you utterly delicious."

Isabella began to scream wildly. "*Help! Someone help us...Please!*"

"No one will hear you down here, child," said Silas.

"You're a monster," said Adele softly, her eyes downcast.

Her uncle smiled warmly. "Not for much longer, child."

Without warning a shudder pushed through Adele and her eyes flew open. A flood of memories, like pages from a book, flipped rapidly through her mind. She recalled being in the storeroom with Isabella and her uncle. Then the floor fell away...the next memory she had was of mumbled voices and movement through the tunnels, the damp walls slipping by. And something else; a flash of light glimpsed through an open door. Inside was a brightly lit room with a pair of glass coffins in the center and a bank of machines along the wall.

Adele gasped. Not coffins—chambers. Two glass chambers!

"I saw it," said Adele, fear coating each word. She looked fiercely at her uncle. "I saw what you've built! It's the chamber Dr. Mangrove dreamed up all those years ago; the missing chapter from his book. I'm right aren't I? When I first read his insane theories about cheating death I thought it was impossible." Adele was shaking her head, her face pale. "It couldn't be true. Mangrove believed a human soul could move between bodies and that awful contraption is how he...how you plan to do it." Tears of anger and helplessness crowded her eyes. How cruel it was to finally understand what her uncle was planning now that it was too late to stop him...and too late to save Milo.

"You're going to steal Milo's body," she whispered. "That's what this is all about, isn't it, Uncle Silas?"

"Steal Milo's *what?*" yelled Isabella, unable to believe what she was hearing.

"It's an evil thing you're doing!" said Adele bitterly. "A horrible, terrible, evil thing!"

"Indeed," agreed Silas. "But utterly brilliant, don't you think? My body is dying, and I need a new one. Dr. Mangrove's genius has made that possible." He raised his hand waving at his nieces. "Farewell, children. Apart from this unfortunate ending, I do hope you enjoyed your time here at Sommerset."

Turning his chair, Silas taxied down the tunnel, leaving a track of bloody tire prints in his wake. The girls could hear their uncle humming contentedly to himself. At the mouth of the tunnel, he stopped suddenly.

"Oh, and don't worry about your parents," he told them. "They will be contacted in a day or two and told that there has been a *terrible* accident: you two inquisitive girls were exploring down in the basement when you accidentally wandered into the wrong tunnel and *oops*—eaten alive by a pack of hungry alligators."

Laughing softly, Silas exited the tunnel with the terrified screams of his nieces ringing in his ears.

Trapped

As Milo crossed the entrance hall he felt it—the eerie silence that had settled around Sommerset like a fog. It was as if the entire island was a deserted ship. Hopping toward the front door, he passed the mangled elevator shaft, swinging his broken leg over the cracked stone floor. He was on a mission to find Moses and make him talk. Whatever secrets the old gardener was holding about Silas Winterbottom, it was time he spoke them aloud.

After all, Adele and Isabella's lives might very well depend on it.

Milo did not believe for one minute that his cousins had been sent home. A rumbling in the very pit of his stomach told him that the girls were still on the island. They were close, he could feel it. But where?

Grabbing the door handle, Milo made a silent vow to do whatever it took to find them. Locked. He tried again. The door would not budge. Milo's breathing began to quicken as it hit him—he was trapped inside Sommerset House. A prisoner.

"Can I help you, Master Milo?" said Bingle from behind him.

Milo turned his head. "Why is this door locked?"

The head butler was carrying a tray containing a pot of tea and a selection of freshly baked biscuits from the kitchen. He cleared his throat. "Well, sir," he said, "your uncle felt it best that you stay indoors. Just for today. It's awful chilly outside."

"Open this door, Bingle," said Milo sharply. "Open it *now!*"

"I'm afraid I can't do that, sir." He noticed Milo glancing off toward the drawing room. "You will find, Master Milo, that all of the doors are locked."

"Where is my uncle?" Milo demanded to know. "I want to see him!"

"The master is taking a meeting in his study," explained Bingle calmly. He walked toward a circular table in the center of the entrance hall. "You do not look at all well, Master Milo. Let me help you back up to your bedroom." Carefully Bingle placed the tray on the table. "Yes, I think that is best. Your uncle will come and see you as soon as he is able."

Bingle turned back to escort the boy upstairs, but he had vanished. Once again, Sommerset House was silent.

Hopping up the narrow staircase, Milo ascended to the second floor of the library. He had been searching a good hour or more, going over every inch of the place looking for the secret compartment. Adele had disappeared before she could tell him the exact location, and Milo knew that if he wanted to find a way into the basement, then he would need the blueprints.

Weaving between the towering bookcases he ran his eyes over every shelf. It had to be here *somewhere*. Turning into the last aisle, Milo immediately noticed the jumble of books still scattered on the ground where Adele had left them. His heart skipped a beat. Adele would never leave books lying around; she cared for them too dearly.

Fast as he could, Milo hopped down the aisle. He saw it immediately. The concealed bookshelf was still wide open. It didn't take long for him to realize that the books scattered on the floor must be the contents of the hidden vault. Milo sifted through the pile looking for the blueprints, coming swiftly to the last tome. *The Science of the Soul* by Dr. Mikal Mangrove. He studied the cover closely. This was the book Adele had told him about.

"The soul is a fascinating thing," said Silas.

Milo gasped, spinning around. The master of Sommerset sat before him. He looked frail, his long hair shielding much of his face, his head bent forward like he was having trouble holding it up.

"I admire your determination, Milo," said Silas softly. "It is a sign of character."

"Where are my cousins?" Milo demanded to know. He thrust the book toward his uncle. "Here's the secret you've been trying so hard to protect—you and *Dr. Mangrove*. I think Adele and Isabella discovered what you were up to, and you removed them just like you remove everything that gets in your way." Milo pushed his crutches away and lunged forward, gripping the armrests of the wheelchair. "You won't get away with this, Uncle Silas!" he shouted. "I won't let you."

"I suspect you are right, child," admitted Silas.

Milo looked into the darkness of his uncle's eyes. They glowed menacingly like two bottomless pits.

"I will not get away with it," said Silas with a faint smile, "but *you* will."

A hand came from behind Milo and pushed a rag into his face, covering his nose and mouth. He struggled to pull the hand away, but the grip was too firm. Rapidly the fumes took effect and Milo's body went limp as he fell into unconsciousness.

Easing the boy's body to the ground, Dr. Mangrove grinned excitedly at Silas.

"Now we can begin."

When the first alligator clawed its way into the tunnel, Isabella's scream tore through the place like an explosion. The beast sniffed the air with hungry curiosity. The scattered chicken and water buffalo soon lured others, exciting their senses. The slick dark beasts gradually moved deeper inside the tunnel.

"*Help us!*" shouted Isabella, her face red with strain. *"Someone help! We're going to be eaten!"*

"No one can hear you," said Adele anxiously, fear stinging her voice. She looked about the tunnel desperately. "There's got to be a way out of this!"

"Then find it, cousin!" screamed Isabella.

Adele noticed a metal grille secured to the ceiling about twenty feet in front of her. She couldn't be sure, but it looked like some sort of gate.

"Look," she said, pointing, "up there—"

"Grrrrrrrrrrr!"

A fierce snarl vibrated down the tunnel. Both girls looked up as a monstrous-looking alligator, some fifteen feet long, moved quickly inside, its thick legs tracking mud along the damp floor. Two smaller alligators that were gathered around a chicken carcass slunk away from the larger beast as it approached. The huge reptile prowled close to the abandoned carcass, then lunged swiftly, its jagged teeth snapping down on the meat, swallowing it whole.

Both girls screamed, pulling wildly on the chains as if they might tear them from the concrete. Adele began to cry, unable to control the fear pumping through her veins. They were going to be eaten alive!

Suddenly the reptile stopped. Its wet eyes slid around, fixing on them.

"It's seen us!" cried Isabella, her voice cracking.

"Shh!" warned Adele. "Be quiet. Don't move."

Both girls were silent. Completely still.

The alligator seemed to lose interest, turning away. Then, without warning, the beast roared, its fierce jaw cracking open. It lunged forward, clawing rapidly toward Adele and Isabella.

The Soul Chamber

Darkness. Darkness everywhere. Then a white light. It stung his eyes. He blinked, lifting his hand to block out the harsh glare...but he couldn't move. He was strapped down. His arms and legs tightly secured.

"Maestro!" he called out. "Maestro, where are you?"

"Relax, Milo," a soothing voice told him.

Gradually his eyes adjusted to the light. Milo looked up and saw a man looming over him—his round, hairless face resembled the moon in orbit. He was smiling, his eyes no more than two small slits, his teeth a putrid yellow.

"I am Dr. Mangrove," he told the boy. "I am here to help you. Do not worry if you feel a little groggy—that is merely the chloroform wearing off."

Chloroform? Milo struggled to make sense of anything. Then gradually the haze began to lift. He tried to get up, straining against the restraints.

"Let me go!" he shouted, struggling in vain. "Let me out of here!"

Although Milo could not see it, he was strapped inside one of two rectangular chambers placed side by side in the underground laboratory. Constructed of thick glass, the chambers were linked by two large pipes locked into a panel of silver valves at the side of the machines. The panel contained numerous small levers and gauges and each had a timer set at 2.00 minutes. At the end of each chamber was a copper test tube attached to a drip that curled into a vent at the base.

"There is no point in struggling," came the familiar voice of his uncle. Unable to see above the chamber, Milo turned his head and saw the jubilant face of Silas Winterbottom peering at him through the thick glass.

"We are pioneers, Milo, and today we make history," he declared passionately. "You see, child, you and I are about to make an exchange. An exchange of souls." He leaned closer to the chamber wall. "I am taking your body, Milo. I sincerely apologize for the condition of the one you are getting in return. I am afraid it is dying. Still, you will not have to live with it for long, so I do not suppose it really matters."

"You're crazy!" Milo shouted. "It's not possible!"

"Oh, but it is," said Silas softly. "Dr. Mangrove has kept his body alive for nearly two hundred years—the man is a genius beyond measure. This magnificent machine you are strapped into is his life's work; he rather poetically calls it the *Soul Chamber*. Once I take my place in the chamber next to you, our souls will be transferred in a matter of minutes." Silas smiled. "I've been paying such close attention to you these past weeks; you probably thought I found you terribly fascinating.

Alas, dear boy, you are rather dull when it's all said and done. The truth is, I needed to observe you carefully so that I could replicate your tedious little personality—thus avoiding any suspicion once your body becomes my own. You should be honored, Milo, you were always my first choice. Your cousins were merely an insurance policy in the event that you proved unsuitable for the transference. Mercifully, Isabella and Adele are no longer needed. In fact, I would imagine that by now they are rather…dead."

Like a wounded tiger, Milo let out a colossal roar, his hot breath fogging up the chamber walls.

"Naturally you hate me." Silas sighed wistfully. "I do not blame you. I am stealing your future, after all. But you must understand that I have to do this. Death is ready for me, but, you see, I am not ready for death. Soon the world will believe I am you, and tomorrow, following the death of Silas Winterbottom, you…that is, *I* will become Sommerset's new heir. It is a shame I could not convince you to publicly accept your role as heir apparent, but fear not. Your change of heart will be perfectly believable."

"You can't do this!" yelled Milo violently. "Let me out of here!"

Silas shook his head. "Never."

As Milo strained to free himself, he spotted Dr. Mangrove from the corner of his eye working busily at a panel of computers lining the far wall. Soon the doctor approached the chamber, carrying a small container of honey-colored liquid, which he carefully poured in the copper test tube.

"We are ready," Dr. Mangrove announced. "Silas, it is time for you to take your place."

Silas closed his eyes. "At last," he whispered.

"I'm afraid I can't let you do that, sir," declared a voice from behind them.

Standing in the doorway holding a long-bladed knife was Mrs. Hammer. Her hand was trembling and the sharp blade flared under the bright lights of the laboratory. She moved toward Silas and the doctor, waving the knife in front of them.

"Mrs. Hammer!" shouted Milo desperately. "I'm in here, Mrs. Hammer!"

"Mercy! Are you hurt, Milo?"

"No." He struck the sides of the chamber. "I just want to get out of this thing!"

"Free the child at once," she ordered, pointing at Silas. "Take him out of that monstrous contraption!"

"Well, well," said Silas brightly, "so you are my assassin. How marvelous! I did not think you had it in you, Mrs. Hammer, cutting the elevator ropes and so on. I am impressed."

"Be quiet!" she snapped. "I don't care what you think of me! When I overheard you and that so-called *doctor* talking about the children like they were animals in a zoo, I decided then and there to stop you. You've done some dreadful things over the years, sir, and much to my shame, I've helped you do them...but I never thought you were capable of *this*. Hurting these dear children who never did you any harm—it's monstrous!"

"Come now, Mrs. Hammer," said Silas, moving slowly toward the housekeeper, "we both know you are not really going to use that knife." He held out his hand. "Give it to me before you hurt yourself, dear lady."

"Perhaps, *sir*, you don't know me as well as you think," declared Mrs. Hammer, her lips forming a snarl. "I don't consider myself a violent woman, but did you know I dreamed up dozens of ways to kill you? Oh, yes. Quiet ways, clever ways, tidy ways. But in the end, I wanted your death to be as black as your heart. That is why I chose the elevator. I cut the cable and prayed that it would become your coffin." Her lips drew together tightly. "But you managed to save yourself…and more's the pity!"

"The knife, Mrs. Hammer," said Silas calmly, moving ever closer. "Give it to me."

"I told you to get back!" she cried, tightening her grip on the knife.

With a flash of steel, Mrs. Hammer swung violently, cutting across the back of Silas's outstretched hand. The flesh sliced open, quickly bleeding a trail along his arm. Silas stared at the wound, transfixed by the sight of his own blood.

"You will not harm one hair on that boy's head," declared Mrs. Hammer firmly. She pointed the blade at Dr. Mangrove. "Free Milo now, Doctor!"

Obediently, Dr. Mangrove hurried toward the chamber, reaching over to unbuckle the first restraint. Just then a series of terrified screams tore through the basement.

Mrs. Hammer instantly recognized the voices.

"Adele!" she cried, looking out toward the tunnels. "Isabella!"

With fury in his black eyes, Silas charged forward, knocking Mrs. Hammer backward with the full force of his wheelchair. She fell to the ground in the corner of the laboratory, the knife slipping out of her hand. Scrambling across the floor, she reached for the blade just as Silas swung down scooping it up. As he pulled away, Mrs. Hammer grabbed his bony wrist, squeezing it fiercely until Silas was forced to drop the knife. She grabbed it, climbing to her feet.

"What have you done to those girls?" she demanded to know. "Which tunnel are they in?"

Thrusting his hand against the back wall of the laboratory, Silas hit a small switch. Without warning, a row of bars shot up from the floor in front of Mrs. Hammer. The thick beams knocked the knife from her hand, sending her plummeting to the ground as the bars rose swiftly to the roof. In seconds, the unconscious housekeeper had been caged in the corner like an animal.

"We have wasted enough time," hissed Silas, turning back to the Soul Chambers. "Let us begin immediately!"

With a hideous grin, Dr. Mangrove turned a gauge on the control panel—a low hum filled the laboratory as the dome-shaped hatch closed over Milo, locking into place.

With the chamber sealed, the boy's screams could no longer be heard.

ℓℓℓℓ

"It's coming for us!" hollered Isabella. *"It's coming!"*

As the gigantic alligator clawed furiously along the damp tunnel, it let out a loud hungry growl revealing rows of jagged teeth. Picking up speed, the beast's tail lashed the tunnel walls as it drew closer to the girls.

"We have to do something!" shouted Adele, her heart pounding like a hammer inside her chest.

Tearing down the tunnel, the alligator was barely ten feet from them when Adele, acting purely on instinct, stepped forward and kicked a large chicken carcass at the alligator. The plucked bird shot into the air and hit the reptile square in the nose with a thump. The dark beast growled, snapping furiously at the chicken, and then dropped from its haunches.

"Good thinking, cousin!" cried Isabella.

"He will try again," said Adele, catching her breath. "You can be sure of it. If only we had something sharp to cut these restraints," she said, pulling roughly at the straps on her wrist.

Isabella let out a squeal. "Cousin...cousin, I may have something!" she cried.

Pulling against the chains, Isabella turned her hips until she was able to slide a hand into her back pocket. Adele watched as an array of stolen property was hastily pulled out—a letter opener followed by a polished gemstone, then two pocket watches, a tie clip, and finally a rather shiny toenail clipper.

"A toenail clipper," gasped Adele. "You stole a *toenail* clipper?"

"It's solid gold!" snapped Isabella as she released the safety latch. "Besides, I only *borrowed* it."

Farther down the tunnel, the large beast turned toward them again, snarling furiously and lashing its tail about. Pushing on its thick stumpy legs, the reptile jumped onto the backs of several other alligators, clawing over them to get at the girls.

He broke into a run.

"Hurry, cousin!" cried Isabella. "Lean toward me so I can free you!"

With trembling hands she began to cut through the thick leather restraints. The predator snapped hungrily, covering more and more ground as the first restraint was cut away. Frantically Adele grabbed a length of chain as the alligator lunged at her legs. She jumped back and swung the chain wildly, lashing the beast's snout. The reptile's flesh split open and it groaned loudly, dropping back.

Without a second to spare, Adele grabbed the clippers from her cousin and cut herself free, then did the same for her cousin. Overcome by fury, Isabella grabbed two large pieces of water buffalo and hurled them at the reptiles.

"Back off, you hideous beasts!" she shouted.

But the beasts did not back off. Instead, as if responding to a silent battle cry, they suddenly charged forward as a pack—dozens of hungry alligators in a battalion bearing down on a common enemy.

Fearing that all hope was lost, Isabella shut her eyes and let out a bloodcurdling roar. It was then that Adele remembered the grille she had spotted earlier.

Realizing it was their only hope, she raced forward, heading straight for the stampeding pack. The beasts pounded the damp tunnel floor, climbing over one another to get the first bite.

"Cousin, come back!" cried Isabella.

Just inches from their hungry jaws, Adele spotted what she was looking for. Swiftly, she pulled on a rusty lever set into the tunnel wall. It resisted her pull, but she gritted her teeth and yanked it down. The steel gate above dropped like a curtain, puncturing one of the alligators through the jaw barely an inch from her foot. The pack of beasts came to a sudden stop, crushing against one another as they hit the storm gate.

Running to her cousin, Isabella hugged her tightly. A mixture of relief and exhaustion overwhelmed them both.

Suddenly Adele pulled away. "Milo," she said. It was all she needed to say.

Nodding in agreement, Isabella grabbed her cousin's hand and together they raced down the darkened tunnel praying they weren't too late.

A Death in the Family

"In just a few minutes you will be reborn," promised Dr. Mangrove as he lowered Silas's frail body into the empty chamber. "As you know, the process is brief. The first minute will prepare your soul for transference. After that, the exchange will happen rapidly. At last you will be free of this dying body."

Silas grabbed the doctor's hand. "I will never forget all that you have done for me, Dr. Mangrove." His eyes pulsed with exhilaration. "And this is just the beginning, dear friend. Next it shall be *your* turn. We will find the panacea and you shall be free. With my fortune and your genius, we will be unbeatable!"

The doctor nodded hungrily.

"And if anything were to go…*astray*," whispered Silas, "you know what to do."

"Plan B," said Dr. Mangrove, setting his patient into the chamber. "I will see to it."

He turned the gauge. The domed hatch began to close over Silas.

"The next time we meet," said the doctor, "you will be Milo Winterbottom."

"Indeed," whispered Silas as the hatch sealed shut. Turning his head, he looked through the thick panels of glass to the second chamber and saw his nephew struggling against the restraints, the veins in his neck bulging. Milo caught sight of his uncle and screamed violently at him. Silas grinned back, basking in the warm glow of victory.

Working above them, Dr. Mangrove quickly set the modulator to the *Ready* position. He entered a ten-digit code and a red button rose from beneath the metallic panel. It glistened under the overhead lights. Dr. Mangrove took one final look over his creation before activating it. In a split second the nuclear generator came to life, triggering the feeder pumps linking the two chambers. The copper test tubes began to spin and the golden elixir snaked its way through the narrow pipe.

The two-minute timer began counting back.

1 min 59 sec

Almost immediately, Milo felt an intense pressure in his brain as the chamber filled with a sweet-smelling gas—it intensified with each passing second until the boy feared his head was about to crack open. Then the air around him began to vibrate, his skin tingling. A pulling sensation gripped his flesh—it felt as if a thousand molecules were tunneling deep under his skin and then bursting out again, taking with it his very life force.

He began to cry out.

1 min 48 sec

The thick pipes pulsated violently, preparing to carry between them the delicate fragments of two souls. Dr. Mangrove's tiny eyes shone like gemstones. It was working!

1 min 40 sec

The pounding of footsteps shook the doctor from his moment of glory. Someone was coming! Lurching toward the laboratory door, he slammed it shut, but a powerful push from outside thrust the door open again, sending Dr. Mangrove tumbling to the ground.

Isabella and Adele burst into the room gasping for breath—they had raced down dozens of identical tunnels searching desperately for the laboratory.

They heard the deep whirl emanating from the two chambers.

The soul transference was already under way!

"Milo!" cried Adele, running to the chamber and peering inside. She let out a horrified scream as she watched her cousin's small body jolt and twitch as if he were being hit with an electric charge.

"How do we stop this?" she yelled at Dr. Mangrove. "Tell us how to stop it!"

"It cannot be stopped. Once the process has begun it is irreversible," said Dr. Mangrove, smoothing down his clothes. He grinned at the girls. "You are too late to save the day."

"Tell us how to shut it down, fathead!" barked Isabella, stomping down hard on the ancient doctor's foot.

Releasing a howl, Dr. Mangrove doubled over in agony. "No!" he spat.

Searching for an off switch, Adele noticed the counter on the control panel.

1 min 21 sec

“We’re running out of time!” she cried.

Working frantically, Isabella and Adele studied the mass of buttons and gauges and pulsating pipes connecting the two chambers. They punched a host of buttons at random. Nothing worked.

1 min 12 sec

“There’s only one thing we can do,” said Adele in utter desperation. “We have to break it open! Quickly, Isabella, when I count to three, push as hard as you can!”

Isabella nodded with grim determination, pressing her hands against the glass chamber.

1 min 04 sec

“One, two, *three!*” yelled Adele.

With every ounce of strength each girl possessed, they pushed against the chamber. It tilted just a fraction, but quickly fell back into place.

“You will not succeed!” mocked Dr. Mangrove, grimacing as he stumbled toward the Winterbottoms. “The chamber is far too heavy for a pair of *little* girls.”

A mixture of anger and desperation rushed through Adele and she lunged at the doctor, kicking him in the shins with every single ounce of strength she possessed. Like a wounded animal, Dr. Mangrove howled wildly, falling to the ground in a tangle.

“We can do this,” she said sternly, returning to the chamber wall. “Milo needs us.”

She signaled to Isabella, and they began to push again. With gritted teeth and trembling arms, the girls threw their entire bodies into the task. The chamber's base began to lift from the ground.

"Harder!" yelled Adele.

They pushed harder, as a series of fierce grunts tore from between their clenched teeth. The chamber lifted from the floor again—higher, this time. Ignoring the pain, they pushed harder still. The chamber began to tilt, the weight of the massive machine lurching away from them.

It was tipping!

"Noooooooo!!" cried Dr. Mangrove, stumbling toward the chamber.

Milo's glass tomb plunged, tearing one of the connecting pipes from Silas's chamber as it toppled to the ground—the glass hatch smashing into a thousand fragments on impact. A roar, like a jet engine, exploded from the generator and a thick wall of smoke billowed out.

Dr. Mangrove slumped to the ground with a look of utter defeat and covered his face.

Moving quickly, Adele and Isabella released Milo from the restraints and pulled his limp body from the wreckage. The shattered glass had caused several cuts on his face and neck and his skin was covered in a film of sticky resin. He lay on the ground, unmoving.

"Milo!" shouted Isabella. "Milo, wake up! Oh, cousin, what if we were too late?"

"We're not too late!" said Adele with certainty. She grabbed

Milo's shoulders and began to shake him. "Milo! Milo, can you hear me?"

Slowly the boy's eyes began to flicker, his dry lips parting as a low groan came from his mouth.

"He's moving!" shouted Isabella. "I told you he would be fine!"

Carefully the girls helped Milo sit up. His eyes opened a little and he looked around at the smoking wreckage of the laboratory.

"Thank you," he said softly, his voice hoarse. "You saved my life—both of you."

"Well, of course we did," said Isabella. "It was very dangerous work, but we are cousins, after all."

Adele looked at Milo carefully. "Do you still feel like *you?*" The thought had crossed her mind more than once—had *any* of Uncle Silas's soul been transferred into Milo before the chamber was destroyed?

Milo considered the question for a moment.

"Well..." he said eventually. "I think I'm still me. It's hard to know for sure."

"Do you have any sudden urge to steal someone's body?" said Isabella matter-of-factly. "Or feed two perfectly wonderful girls to a pack of hungry alligators?"

"No," said Milo with a grin. "None at all."

"It's settled then," said Isabella with certainty. "You are not possessed."

But Adele was not so easily convinced.

"That night," she said carefully, watching Milo, "when I snuck in through your bedroom window. Do you remember the first thing I said after I climbed down off the windowsill?"

Milo did not answer immediately. He looked at his cousin gravely, shaking his head. "No," he said softly. "You didn't climb off the windowsill, I grabbed your arm and pulled you down. Remember?"

"Yes!" cried Adele, the relief bringing a wide smile to her face.

"So," said Milo, grinning back at her, "did I pass the test?"

"It's official," declared Adele. "You are not Uncle Silas."

Milo's smile slipped away as he looked over at the remaining chamber where his uncle lay—the generator was still whirling and the remaining pipe flailed around like a serpent, spewing the elixir gas into the air.

"Is he…dead?" asked Milo.

"I don't know," said Adele. She gulped. "There's only one way to find out."

With the help of his cousins, Milo got to his feet and together they crossed to the chamber. They looked down through the hatch. Silas's eyes were closed, his thin body completely still.

"Looks dead to me," said Isabella.

"I think you're right," said Adele with a sigh of relief.

Just then Silas's eyes sprung open, his eyelids flipping up like a slot machine. They were as black and vibrant as ever, rippling with fury. His bony hands thrust against the hatch, pushing violently on the glass.

The children recoiled, their screams filling the room.

"I told you he was alive!" cried Isabella.

Lunging forward, Silas pressed his face to the chamber's wall and peered out at the children, his ghostly face fuelled with rage, his teeth bared like the fangs of a wolf. Realizing Silas would never stop as long as he lived, Milo reached for the flailing pipe still connected to the chamber. As he did, a pair of hands clamped around his neck, throwing him against the wall. Milo tumbled to the ground, his head thumping the wall. Dazed, the boy looked up and saw Dr. Mangrove standing over the chamber, his hands spread across the glass.

"All is well, old friend," he said. "I will have you out in no time."

The doctor worked rapidly, pressing buttons and turning gauges. "The transference was working," he said tensely, stealing glances at Silas. "Your soul was shifting! Do not worry, I can rebuild the other chamber in a matter of days and then we can try again."

"Excuse me, Doctor?" said Isabella.

Furiously, Dr. Mangrove looked around, and as he did, two things happened: Isabella delivered a spectacular kick to the doctor's already battered shin and then Adele and Milo bolted from behind, ramming into him like a bull. The waxy old monster bellowed as he flew toward the ground, tumbling in a heap.

"Look!" cried Adele.

The hatch was opening! Adele began to furiously push the buttons, *any* buttons, trying to shut the hatch. Nothing seemed to work. She coughed as the gases spewing from the pipe rose toward her. A pair of bony claws slammed against the glass and Silas released a violent hiss. She screamed.

"We have to close it!" shouted Isabella, desperately trying to push down on the hatch.

Steam began to escape from the chamber as it slowly opened.

Milo reached again for the pipe, which was flailing about under the chamber. Acting on instinct, he pushed it into the empty valve, looping the poisonous gases back into the hatch.

"Stand back!" shouted Milo, pulling his cousins away.

Immediately the chamber filled with thick plumes of yellow smoke. It began to shake, pallid fumes whirling around Silas, churning with increasing ferocity. The thick glass panels started to crack.

"It's going to explode!" shouted Isabella.

As the children looked on, their uncle's body was lifted by the whirlwind, and began to spin rapidly in the frenetic churn. The master of Sommerset's shallow cry was swallowed up in a torrent, his body a blur as the yellow smoke frosted the cracked glass walls.

Just as quickly the generator stopped, the chamber's violent shaking coming to an abrupt end. In front of the massive computer terminal Dr. Mangrove had cut the power source, bringing to an end the mini-tornado.

Pushing the children aside, he rushed at the chamber, releasing the hatch. Plumes of hideous smelling yellow smoke filled the room. As it cleared, Dr. Mangrove leaned forward, peering inside.

"Silas!" he cried.

The children surrounded the chamber. In the place where their uncle had been lying was a mound of fine chalky powder. It was difficult to believe, at first, that the almighty Silas Winterbottom could be rendered a pile of dust.

"He has been incinerated," said the doctor softly.

A loud moan from the corner of the room diverted the children's attention.

"Mrs. Hammer!" shouted Milo as he glimpsed the caged housekeeper for the first time. Struggling, Milo and Isabella tried to dislodge the bars, but it was no use. A rather groggy Mrs. Hammer directed Adele to the hidden switch beside the door, and the iron cage dropped swiftly back into the floor.

"Oh, Milo," cried Mrs. Hammer, "thank goodness you're all right!"

"I'm fine, Mrs. Hammer," said Milo, squeezing her hand. "And thank you for trying to save me. You are very brave!"

"Oh, nonsense," laughed Mrs. Hammer.

Suddenly Adele gave a shout.

Dr. Mangrove was nowhere to be seen. He had fled the laboratory, disappearing down the labyrinth of tunnels. On a hunch Milo hopped over to the smoking ruins of his uncle's chamber and looked inside. A chill raced up his spine.

The powdery remains of Uncle Silas had vanished.

The Last Will and Testament of Silas Winterbottom

The Winterbottoms sat in the conservatory of Sommerset House waiting for Whitlam to arrive. As soft sunlight splashed across the black-and-white checkered floor, each member of the family sat quietly, still haunted by the events of the past few days.

Silas was dead. He had lured the children to Sommerset with a wicked plan to steal a soul and now he was dead. Milo's body still ached from his time in the Soul Chamber, but as he sat close to his grandfather he felt better than he had in weeks. The maestro had jumped on a plane the minute he found out what had happened to his grandson, and he had not left the boy's side since.

There had been no sign of Dr. Mangrove since his escape from the basement. The police seemed to believe that he had been eaten by Silas's alligators—his shredded coat was found near a tunnel leading directly into the swamp and there was blood on it.

The doctor was not the only person to disappear from Sommerset—Bingle had fled in the dead of night, and no one had heard from him since.

When Whitlam finally entered the conservatory he was forced to step over Thorn, who was lying across the doorway. He was quickly followed by Mrs. Hammer carrying a pitcher of lemonade and a freshly baked pie.

"Oh, cousin, this is it," whispered Isabella, tapping Adele's hand. "We are about to become very rich...very, *very* rich!"

Adele frowned. "Us? Are you crazy? Uncle Silas has left everything to Milo—that's the whole reason he wanted to steal his body, remember?"

"Well, I know that," said Isabella crossly. "But don't you see? Milo won't want any part the estate—especially after what Uncle Silas did. And that means Sommerset will go to us!"

"What makes you think that?" said Adele.

"It's simple really," declared Isabella. "Milo knows how much we both love Sommerset, and let us not forget—we saved the poor orphan's life. He will feel it is his duty to hand Uncle Silas's fortune over to us. Just you wait and see!"

Adjusting his spectacles, Whitlam shuffled to the front of the room and stood before a bank of large windows overlooking the rose gardens.

"Well, children, you have certainly had a holiday to remember, haven't you?" he said, winking at Milo (who gave the lawyer a smile in return). "On a serious note, I feel nothing but regret for my role in bringing you to Sommerset. If I had known what Silas was up to...well, I would have stopped him myself! You showed great courage—all of you—standing up to him and stopping his diabolical scheme. Congratulations all around, I say!"

As Mrs. Hammer, Rosemary, and the maestro applauded enthusiastically, Whitlam pulled a large envelope from inside his coat. "Now then, let us get down to business. Silas's will." He sighed heavily. "In fact, your uncle's wishes are very simple really, and however objectionable I might find some of the contents—it is perfectly legal, and therefore I am duty bound to enforce it."

The whole room watched expectantly as Whitlam broke the seal and opened the will. He cleared his throat.

"Now then...the great bulk of Silas Winterbottom's estate, including Sommerset and all other assets and money has been left to Milo Winterbottom."

All eyes fell upon Sommerset's new heir.

"Congratulations, Milo," said Rosemary warmly.

"Thank you," said Milo, shaking his head. "But I don't want it."

"My boy," said the maestro, looking tenderly at his grandson, "you should take some time to think about it, yes? This is a great thing you are giving up."

"I have thought about it, Maestro," explained Milo. "I don't want Sommerset—I never did. The truth is..." He turned around, facing his cousins. "I want Adele and Isabella to have it. After what they did for me, it's the least I can do."

Isabella jumped to her feet and flew at Milo, hugging him brutally.

"Oh, cousin, you are too kind! Thank you, thank you! What a sweet little orphan you turned out to be!"

Still sitting quietly in her chair, Adele felt fresh tears slide down her freckled cheeks. She caught Milo's eye and mouthed the words "Thank you, Milo."

After all that they had been through together, it was all she needed to say.

"Who'd have thought it? Sommerset has *two* heirs!" said Rosemary, as she guzzled a slice of freshly baked peach pie.

"I'm afraid not," said Whitlam gravely. "The terms of Silas's will state that if Milo refuses the estate then Silas's fortune will become the property of...Dr. Mikal Mangrove."

Gasps were heard around the conservatory.

"What?" hollered Isabella. "You're *kidding* me, right?"

"I wish I was," answered Whitlam. "And that is not the worst of it. In the event that Milo does not choose to become the next heir of Sommerset, several other clauses in the will come into effect. The first is that two hundred thousand dollars will be paid to Adele's mother, Prudence Winterbottom—on the condition that Adele is sent to Ratchet's House until her eighteenth birthday."

"Ratchet's House!" shouted Adele. She tried to get up, but her legs turned to jelly. Dropping, she fell back in the chair. Silas had taken her greatest fear and brought it to life.

"There is more," continued Whitlam somberly. "The second clause concerns Miss Isabella. Your uncle kept a detailed dossier of your activities in London over the past year." The old lawyer paused awkwardly. "I refer to the theft of valuable objects from the homes of your school friends. This dossier is to be delivered to the London police authorities. I have no doubt that there is enough evidence in there to have both you and your father locked away for a very long time. I am sorry."

Isabella tried to remain as calm as possible, but naturally it did not work.

"This is an *outrage!*" she cried. "A travesty! Why, if Uncle Silas wasn't already dead, I'd kill the old bag of bones all over again!"

"I knew my brother was a swine, but this is inhuman!" said Rosemary, passing out tissues to Adele and Isabella. "Now, Whitlam, am I right in assuming that if Milo *does* become Sommerset's new heir…then none of these awful clauses will be carried out?"

Whitlam nodded. "That's right." He smiled sadly at Milo, who looked completely dazed by the turn of events. "Your uncle was prepared to do whatever it took to persuade you."

The boy was trapped. Even in death Silas was controlling them. What choice did he have but to accept the mantle of Sommerset's new heir? He could hardly believe he was thinking such a thing! But if he didn't, what would become of his Adele and Isabella? Not to mention Dr. Mangrove. If that evil genius was still alive, he must never gain access to Sommerset. Who knew what diabolical inventions he could build with Silas's fortune?

"All right," said Milo, as a deep unease swelled within him. "I will do what Uncle Silas wanted. I am the new heir of Sommerset."

A scream tore across the room. It was Mrs. Hammer. She jumped to her feet and ran to the large windows.

"Moses!" she cried, pointing toward the large evergreen oak tree just beyond the rose gardens. "He just fell from that tree! The branch snapped and he fell!"

They rushed from the drawing room, through the entrance hall, and out into the rose garden.

"Over here!" Isabella shouted as she ran between the stone columns at the edge of the rose garden.

"Quick!" she screamed suddenly. "Somebody call the doctor—Moses is badly hurt!"

The old gardener was flat on his stomach, his calloused fingers clawing at the dirt as he dragged his body away from the oak tree.

"Moses, stop!" cried Milo. "You mustn't move!"

Ignoring the warnings, Moses clawed at the ground, pulling himself onto the soft green grass of the rose gardens. His shattered legs dragged behind him like two bags of coal.

"Where are you going, Moses?" said Rosemary desperately. "Please, don't move until help arrives!"

Groaning, Moses pulled himself along the trellised archway and stopped beside a bed of red roses. Then he plunged his fingers into the dirt.

"What's he doing?" said Isabella.

"Moses, what is it?" Milo asked, throwing his crutches to the ground and dropping down beside the gardener. He put his hand on the old man's back. "Moses?"

"I do hope the ambulance hurries up!" said Mrs. Hammer fearfully.

It was Adele who solved the mystery. She peered over Rosemary's shoulder and looked down at the garden bed.

"They're letters," she said. "I think he's writing something!"

When Moses was done, his eyes closed, his body deflating into the soft grass like a punctured tire.

Milo looked down at the rose bed and saw what was written in the soil.

DIG.

Without actually making a decision to do it, Milo plunged his hands into the dirt.

Sommerset

A rusted copper box buried under a bed of red roses and caked in decades of mud and dirt was resurrected from the gardens of Sommerset. Once again, the Winterbottoms gathered together in the conservatory waiting for Whitlam, trying to come to terms with the blackest day in Sommerset's history. Moses was dead. He had drawn his last breath in the very gardens he had tended for so many years.

The police examined the branch that had caused him to plunge from the tree. They were certain it had been tampered with, sawed down so that it would break when Moses stood upon it. One of the gardeners overheard young Knox telling Moses that the master wanted him to trim the evergreen oak that very day. Then Mrs. Hammer recalled Silas having a meeting with Knox in his office right after he intercepted the note Moses wrote to Milo promising him the truth about his uncle. When the police questioned Knox in his quarters, the boy quickly turned to jelly and confessed everything. Silas had offered him the head gardener's job in exchange for doing away with Moses. The young gardener was arrested and taken away.

In the conservatory at the foot of Silas's empty chair, Thorn kept a vigil as if he were awaiting his master's return. Isabella sat on the floor near the beast, stroking his long back, while Adele picked nervously at her fingers and tried as hard as she could not to think about Moses. Naturally, that was all she *could* think about.

The maestro, who had been talking with the police, returned to the conservatory and sat down next to his grandson just as Whitlam made his entrance.

"This has been a day of great tragedy," said Whitlam, scratching at his curly white hair, "and great revelation. My colleagues and I have thoroughly examined the contents of the buried box. I have in my hand two documents. One is a letter from Moses; the other is the final will of Lady Cornelia Bloom."

Puzzled looks were exchanged around the room.

"Well, go *on*, then!" snapped Isabella impatiently. "What does it say?"

"Yes, well," said Whitlam. "I should first make it clear that we have conducted extensive handwriting analysis of Lady Bloom's letters and documents—the will is authentic. As such, Silas's will is no longer valid."

Everybody in the room seemed to gasp at the same time.

"Lady Bloom wrote a new will just a few days before her death," continued Whitlam. "The letter Moses left makes it very clear that Lady Bloom had grown concerned about Silas's behavior—he had become controlling and obsessed with Sommerset. He refused to allow Lady Bloom's family and friends to visit the island and kept Lady Bloom a virtual prisoner. According to Moses, she feared for her life, which is why she left a copy of the new will in his possession—in case anything should happen to her. It was for this reason that Moses sent his son Ezra with her on the day she was to deliver this new will to her lawyers in town. She did not tell Silas what she was doing. However, Moses saw him walking into the forest with an ax in the early hours of that morning. Lady Bloom's car hit a tree that had mysteriously fallen across a sharp bend in the road—the police believed the branch had been deliberately cut, but they couldn't prove it. As we know, Lady Bloom was killed instantly, and the boy suffered severe brain injuries requiring lifelong medical care. Being a cunning fox, Silas agreed to take care of all the boy's medical expenses on the condition that Moses kept his mouth shut about everything. Moses never let on that he had a copy of Lady Bloom's will…until today."

"Heavens above!" said Rosemary, shaking her head. "What a tale! But then, nothing my brother has done would surprise me now. So, Whitlam, here is the million-dollar question—who did Lady Bloom leave Sommerset to?"

"Yes, *who?*" said Isabella anxiously. Murder, secret wills, blackmail—she found the whole thing utterly, tragically romantic!

"Well," said Whitlam, "that's a very good question. It was Lady Bloom's wish that once both she and your uncle were gone, the estate and all of its assets should go to the youngest generation of Blooms and Winterbottoms." The old lawyer grinned. "And as Lady Bloom has no living relatives, that means Sommerset now belongs to Adele, Isabella, and Milo Winterbottom!"

The three Winterbottom children looked at each other wide-eyed and slack jawed. Could it really be true—Sommerset was to be shared by all *three* of them? The answer was yes! Naturally Adele and Isabella were elated, hugging each other and jumping about the place, but Milo did not react.

"Did you hear, my boy?" said the maestro, putting an arm around him. "Just a few hours ago you tried to give Sommerset away, and now it has come back to you again. Fate is trying to tell you something, yes? Maybe now you will listen to it."

"So, Milo," said Adele rather nervously. "Sommerset is ours to share…what do you think?"

"I think…I think Uncle Silas would hate the idea of Sommerset being shared by *three* Winterbottoms. It would drive him crazy. Well, crazier." Milo smiled shyly and stood up, joining his cousins in front of the fireplace. "I think it's perfect!"

That night the island has its first real celebration in years. Every member of the household gathered in the ballroom to hear the maestro play his violin as Rosemary and Mrs. Hammer read a poem in honor of Moses. Then the children gathered outside in the garden and lit a candle for the old gardener, wishing him well on his final journey home. They laughed and talked through the night, making plans for the bright future that seemed to stretch out before them, and as the sun began to rise over the island, the whole family raised their glasses to Lady Cornelia Bloom, thanking her for the gift of Sommerset.

EPILOGUE

From behind a cover of thick vines and cypress trees he watched them at play in the gardens of Sommerset. His eyes, small and bright, studied the Winterbottom children with jealous fascination. They had everything he required—health…youth…fortune.

He looked up at the full moon. It was late. Clutching the cylinder containing the powdery remains of his benefactor, Silas Winterbottom, the ancient doctor turned away and headed back into the depths of the darkened forest.

He had work to do.

ACKNOWLEDGMENTS

This tale was inspired by a book entitled *Aunt Jane's Nieces* written nearly a century ago. I loved the story so much that I set out to write a new version of this delightfully old-fashioned book and everything was going along swimmingly until the young Winterbottoms and their revolting uncle hijacked the story. Suddenly I found myself writing a far more sinister story involving deadly reptiles, murderous villains, a secret assassin, and three young cousins fighting for their very lives. Naturally, I was thrilled!

Despite the change of direction, it was the magic of L. Frank Baum that inspired me, after a lengthy spell in the wilderness, to get back to the keyboard and try again. And so I thank him.

I owe a huge thank-you to the entire team at Sourcebooks Jabberwocky, but most especially to Rebecca Frazer for all her efforts on behalf of this book. Thanks also to Troy Cummings for his brilliant illustrations. Finally, a very special thank-you to my agent Ann Behar, whose boundless optimism and tenacity have made my literary dreams come true.

ABOUT THE AUTHOR

Stephen M. Giles lives near the beach in Sydney. He has worked as a film classifier and a market researcher, but these days he spends most of his time wandering around his imagination—which is where he met the Winterbottoms.